www.finishinglinepress.com

Colleen's Count

a novella by

Rick Henry

Finishing Line Press
Georgetown, Kentucky

Colleen's Count

Publisher: Leah Maines

Editor: Christen Kincaid

Cover Art: Dana Henry—*Ledger*, assemblage, 2020

Author Photo: C A Hill Photo

Cover Design: Elizabeth Maines McCleavy

Order online: www.finishinglinepress.com
also available on amazon.com

Author inquiries and mail orders:
Finishing Line Press
P. O. Box 1626
Georgetown, Kentucky 40324
U. S. A.

Sweet Boo

Wednesday, August 16th (1933)

Her baby girl, Robbie, in the passenger seat of a 1931 Buick Coupe, laughing wide, eyes skyward, filled with summer. Mimi Goncourt giggling from the driver's seat, breaking up from the river, past Musil's, past Marlene's. Stopped at the intersection. Waiting for the green. Robbie laughing. Mimi all teeth and stealing glances. All of this as Colleen settles on the bench, her own smile at her baby girl as she shifts the pillow she'd brought from home, from the divan, to save her back from its twinges, its pressure on her sides, up under her ribs, and around to the front. Baby girl. William Jr. is his own kind of special, barely a twinge of guilt there, but Robbie? Her ghost child, jostling belly to spine, bouncing through her back and against the seat in the Limited as it careened, tires against the ruts. What William never knew.

The light cycles to green. Colleen lifts a hand to wave, but Robbie hasn't seen her. Colleen's surprised that Mimi's driving. Mimi doesn't have a license. Nor does Colleen know where she found the Coupe, unless it is Gaston Louÿs's. If so, it has a large dent on the driver's side door. Kicked by a French draft—shod. Nearly punched through the metal. The Coupe bumbles over the railroad tracks, up the slight rise, over, and out of sight. The license plate, black on yellow, is from '31. Two years out of date.

All of this as Colleen settles on the bench, in the square, with its fountain, its clock, and twenty-four new chestnuts. Complements of the WPA. She's angled where she settles, forty-five degrees to the intersection of Main, Pine, and Pleasant. Across Main, Greer Tennant's law office, above Tennant, Dank's insurance, above Dank, Westcroft's collection agency. One building up, Grambly's First National. Directly through the intersection, the Federated Department Store, newly owned and renamed, manikins and racks of dresses on display through the plate glass. One of Robbie's friends is a window dresser charged with keeping the stilled bodies clothed with summerwear. A sale. Fall on the horizon. Federated trying to compete with Woolworths. Across Pine, Komár's American Theater, closed until further notice. Until Saturday. Komár will reopen with *Three Who Loved*—Saturday matinée. *Hard to Handle* in the evening. He's on his way to Rome for a new projector. A loan. His voice'd dropped when he'd said from whom, and so she'd lost it under his accent, under his mustache. She adjusts her skirt. Stretches the cotton downward from the knees, forty-five buttons down the front, waist to hem, single clasp in the back. Tips her hat. To protect herself from the sun. 7:55 by the town clock behind her. Crosses her legs at the ankles. Pulls the collars of her jacket closer. Still chilly. A Hudson pulls up to the light, muffler overpowering the low bubble from the middle of the square.

Wednesday. August 16th. She was supposed to have settled herself on the 14th, but for the weather. Pencil ready. Steno pad open. Town clock at 7:58. The Hudson rumbles off, leaving a sudden squeal of children floating rubber ducks in the fountain. Robbie's squeal when she first touched a piglet. William long gone. Patrick not yet on the horizon, himself newly married and already restless. Colleen, William Jr., and Robbie at the farm. Her father talking potatoes. Her mother wondering why her three-year-old granddaughter hadn't yet touched a piglet. William Jr. running in a tight circle, arms extended, pretending he was an aeroplane, wishing he had four arms so he could be a biplane. Colleen flushes, heat rising quickly to sweaten her forehead, a chill following just as quickly.

Only three automobiles in the first few minutes, only three heading out east Main, over the railroad tracks and over the rise. She marks them each with a slash. All three Fords, if anyone should ask. She yawns. Still tired from a night of poor sleep. Week of. Month of poor sleep. Fitful. Up a dozen times. Trying not to wake Robbie as she stumbles through the dark. Another slash. And another as Marty Waller's Oldsmobile turns right and trundles the tracks. Odd how little improvement in shocks over nearly twenty years. She assumes Marty Waller is driving. Marty Waller. Coarse as coarse can be. Slash. A Ford. Telling Emma she needed to free the Homer twins. Slash. The bell in the church tower welcomes eight o'clock. Six minutes behind the town clock.

Hollis opens the front door to the First National. Behind him, the young men have treble-checked their tills. Hollis wouldn't hire Tingle Hope. Women can't count.

Three more across the tracks and over the rise. Eight.

The Limited's shocks were something awful. But William? William was smooth, so smooth that she wouldn't even know what he'd said and she'd suddenly be taken up in it all. Wouldn't even know who asked, whether it was Charlotte or Colleen because his eyes…. Of course it was Charlotte. William had been with Lorraine then. Driving out with Charlotte and Colleen in the back with the wind in their hair. Her mother used to warn that it looked like there was something all tousled like that, but there wasn't until later. The wind. She could always use the wind to explain the tangles. William wouldn't even need to explain, just smile at her mother and she'd stop worrying. It's hard for a mother to stop worrying. Buicks have such soft seats now, not like the Oldsmobile. The Limited.

Colleen feels her cheeks flush, raises her pencil hand to undo the top button of her blouse. Pauses. Thinks to Marty Waller. To Emma. To Betty Boop. To Desiré. The flush passes, imperceptible under the light blush. The light turns green. Slash slash slash slash. Squeal from the fountain. Ford. Buick. Ford. Oldsmobile. Up from the river and over the rise. Katherine Rank has a new hat. Lime. It doesn't suit her color. Colleen adjusts her pillow. Twists at the neck to the clock. 8:08.

She might have loved that car more than William if it could talk. "Don't need a smooth talker, just a smooth ride," Charlotte had tittered as they'd arrived, swirl of dust, at Houlton Falls. Before the war, Charlotte laughed like that, tittering behind her hand. Colleen catches herself, thinks it might have been her own laugh back then. Later, after the war, Robbie in the back and the windows down and her hair whipping and her eyes skyward and full with summer, Colleen's laugh had deepened, grown tentative, apologetic, angry. She thinks how hard it is for a mother to stop worrying, to stop thinking about Robbie in the front seat, to stop thinking about Danny Barton smooth-talking over the roar or thrum or pop of whatever car his father's let him drive from the lot. His father and the road they're planning. Thinks to Hollis as a Chevrolet passes—uses her pencil to scratch the back of her neck. Hollis is right. Women can't count.

Smooth as William was, he couldn't take the big bumps. The bumps that counted.

The children continue splashing about the fountain. Colleen thinks she recognizes Hadley's daughter, Kenna, calling out to her three-year-old. Named her Sairy. Ancestral. Maternal. Colleen feels a wisp of a breeze whiffle her bangs. Warmer already. Someone had told her it was going to be warm. She lets her jacket slide from her shoulders. The stitch in her side prevents her from turning other than to allow her to see the water flying about. She reminds herself to talk to Hadley. Today. Maybe tomorrow. Definitely by tomorrow. She uncrosses her ankles, bends forward, and frees the bottom two buttons in the hem of her skirt, then sits back into her pillow.

Even for everything after, they had been glorious days. She imagines the straight stretch, from town out past the chicken factory where they took out the turns in the road. People'd said they could hear the dynamite in town, dynamite straightening the world, smoothing the world. She closes her eyes, missing one two three four five as she recalls the excitement, the straight and wide and freed from the pocks and ruts, from horses and wagons. Imagines the Limited, cream-in-my-coffee colored, top down, imagines him pressing the accelerator, imagines his foot squeezing itself to the floor, imagines bracing herself against the speed. It'd start with the bridge and just go, the feel of it in the stomach, a scream just waiting to be let out, in the stomach then up and up and out into the night and there was nothing but the dark and the flash of road and the rush of it all. Some nights it was just a scream in the dark. He'd turn the headlights off and everything would disappear, the sky, the road, him, everything, and it'd just be a scream braced against the night. Hard for mothers not to worry? Mothers didn't know. They didn't know about automobiles. They had nothing to worry about. Feel the scream. It'd be there ready to burst while he would be talking, talking about anything, anything at all, about the Limited mostly and where it could take him, where it could take them, Buffalo, Chicago, St. Louis, even California, said that was no problem, liveries all the way to the Pacific, just need a trunk full with tires, tubes. But that was early on. They'd figured out the tires, he'd said, by the time they went to the Falls, figured them out so that they could go to California. He painted that nice. Summer, sunshine, always driving into the sinking sun.

Colleen opens her eyes to the roar of a Packard Twin Six. Herman. He'd been talking about a DeLuxe. Once a Packard always a Packard. He heads on down to the bridge. Out of sight. Out of hearing. She wonders about Herman. Wonders why he isn't at work slogging through the easement papers. Wonders about his parents. Who names a baby Herman?

William had her ready. Sunshine. Ocean. Paradise. But no cumbrances. "No cumbrances," he'd said. "Can't cumbrance the Oldsmobile." It had taken a while, but she'd figured what he'd meant. Taken a while. She should have known after Lorraine. After Molly. If she'd been forced to say why…but she knows now she'd known. Hiding William Jr. under sackcloth as long as she could. He must have known, too, with his "no cumbrances" so early on.

She looks to her steno pad. She's checked another half-dozen without thinking. Over the tracks and over the rise. Sun growing warmer on the back of her neck. The paving is foolhardy. The Y at Stuarts—the left fork a half mile, to Barton's Used Cars and the drive-in beyond, the right fork on to Rome. Clem could use the help. Maybe Robbie could do the holding, measuring, now that the James boy has been assigned the sewage tank. "All that education gone to waste." Hinkley thinks it's funny enough to repeat once a day. Herman, one desk down, grimaces once a day over the latest foreclosure. Tax rolls. She tastes the tiniest bit of bile. Baby girl. Robbie wouldn't leave Marlene for Clem. She hadn't liked him when Colleen had him to dinner two years ago. Hadn't liked him when he'd taken Colleen and Robbie to the Gap for a day. He'd talked about dynamiting the bedrock to straighten out the road as it curved over and around the riffles. He'd said that. "Riffles." Showing off. Showing himself out the door. Riffles and kames. William Jr. then, thinks Colleen. He knows a number or two. He needs steady work. Colleen's surprised he hadn't come out funny with all the jostling. Out of sorts. He'd done a number on her spinal cord.

A 1927 Packard Roadster runs the light, a dull thrum from the river to an even duller roar as Danny Barton accelerates, no doubt another test drive for his father. Convertible. White top folded back. Cream and tan body, like William's Limited. Took Robbie in it to *A Shriek in the Night* last Friday. At least it was better than *Jekyll and Hyde*. T'would have been better this Saturday—*The Death Kiss* and *Laughter in Hell*. Komár might be reading her mind. Another six slashes and there'll be a hundred.

Cumbrances. Lorraine came out alright. Desiré had taken care of her. Lorraine made William drive them to Muck Road on the canal in Rome. But it was Desiré who'd taken care of her after. Swept her up to The Hollow. Desiré Renault. Mrs. Renault. William later called her Mademoiselle Renault. Mlle. Renault. She's never had a husband that Colleen knows of. She does have more buttons on her dresses than anyone could imagine. Hundreds. Hundreds of buttons. Colleen's hand rises, unconsciously, to one of her own and frees it. Lorraine had been a hard case. All she could do to keep everything in place in the front seat while Charlotte and Colleen were screaming in the back. William would be talking about anything—smugglers, mushroom soil, spark plugs, anything, but about the Limited mostly. He'd called Charlotte a spark plug. Lorraine'd laughed. Horse laugh. She hadn't belonged in an automobile. Didn't have the speed. Not then. Should have still been riding the cart and wagon. Mothers didn't have to worry with the cart and wagon.

Desiré'd said otherwise. She'd said you could drop the reins and ride the ruts. She'd said it just like that. "Drop the reins and ride the ruts." Desiré with an accent at the end. Because she was accentuated, William'd say. Colleen tries sighing, but the stitch catches her mid-exhale. She doesn't know that it suited. Of course it suited, but not how anyone might think. She tries sighing again, a softer sigh testing the stitch against her rib. Wonders again what parents think about when naming their children. Perhaps Desiré changed her name. Desiré Renault. She makes a note to ask her. She thinks to Muck Road, the smell of the canal. Sewage. Lorraine leaving William after Desiré had helped Molly "take the drive." That was four months after Lorraine, but not to Muck Road, no, Desiré had taken Molly north. Dúil. Lorraine telling Colleen to watch him. To watch herself. He'd never written those miles in his book. They weren't "riding out." Neither were the miles to Niagara, she thinks. Neither were the miles to Niagara. At least those were recorded.

William had known about Renaults. The cars. French racing cars. He'd said you couldn't buy one, but he'd seen one racing the Rome-Avalon road. Avalon. If ever a town was badly named. He'd pronounced it "re-know" like you could see it again. But he'd said it'd never happen. One look, maybe a half a look, a glance, or something out of the corner of your eye, would be all you'd get before it disappeared. That fast. Not over the horizon, *into* the horizon. Colleen scooches slightly, adjusting her back against the pillow. She doesn't believe for a minute that a racing car could ride the ruts. The Rome-Avalon road is a bumpy ride. No chance there was ever a race there. No chance anyone could raise enough interest to have it paved. William'd said a Renault needed special gas. Gas you couldn't get at an ordinary livery. It also needed a special set of wrenches to fix it. Two seater—no back seat at all. Desiré wouldn't have changed her name to a French racing car. She doesn't have an accent, either. Colleen opens another button on her blouse. Crosses, uncrosses her ankles. Leans forward into her stitch and frees another three buttons up from the hem of her skirt. She can't recall how many buttons in the Limited. Deep buttoning. Front seats and back. Arm rests as well. William'd used a boot polish to keep the shine, a polish from Australia, he'd boasted, low hushes about where he'd found it. It'd softened the leather, but the seats were still nearly as hard as the park bench, worse with the bumps. The memory of the smell of that polish rises, catches, nausea. She had been careful. She'd "watched him," as her mother would have said. Thought she'd been careful. Desiré taking Molly north, while Colleen cramped behind the potato shed at her parents' farm, cramped and swallowed screams. Held herself tight, together. The twinge under her ribs is from the memory. The wince pinching her eyes is from the twinge.

To slash or not to slash. Her hand hovers before rising to brush a mosquito from her neck, to adjust the rayon pulling against her shoulder. A two-seater turns left from Pleasant to the tracks to outer Main. A Franklin Roadster. Alfred Tennant driving. Heading to the rise and around-the-block down to Water Street, the bridge, and out past Russell's Corners, turning here, turning toward Rome, as if everyone doesn't know what he's about. Colleen doesn't know how the Roadster handles ruts, but it can't be too well. Skinny tires. Tennant drives out once a day. When they asked Colleen to do the counting, they thought she'd only see numbers. They didn't know that she'd see Alfred Tennant heading toward Russell's Corners. They didn't know that she'd see Georgia Howe taking a left onto Pleasant, followed by a quick right into the alley, to spend forty minutes, before backing her way out because the alley dead-ends. For Deliveries Only. They didn't know that she'd see Eben Rooke driving with Benny Gray out to outer Main, to the Cheese Factory, minutes after Lorraine turned to drive around the block to Belle's. They have two cars. A '29 Cord and a Packard Coupe. Believe it. Two. Lorraine came out alright. Better than alright. She makes Eben drive the Cord.

Colleen runs her nails elbow to shoulder and back. They say that *komár* means "mosquito." She doesn't believe it. Some bites don't scratch.

Violet Gilmor. Slash.

All they knew was they wanted the highway money running through the state. The lawyers and all them in Albany buying up the world, and Grambly and Tennant and Rooke wanted a little piece of it. A little paving outside of town to bring in the customers, two miles out where they'd bought over seven hundred acres from Tennant's grandfather, the entire dairy farm, just out far enough that the zoning doesn't count and they can set up a whole new downtown just the way they want. They'd bought the district's representative in the State Assembly, paid him for a piece of the pie, a stretch of pavement. They'd lamented the coming of Woolworths. Apoplexy at the coming of Federated. Now, in a turnabout, building a road to nowhere. Give them a reason to drive. As if anyone needs a reason. Eben's just dumb enough not to figure out that all of those cows aren't going to be filling his tanks at the dairy. They wanted that. Grambly wants to know what the best automobile is so that he can build a dealership. People need automobiles, not Barton's junk, he'd said. Said people want to drive someplace to shop. They don't want to walk downtown. Nobody wants to walk. Ellen Mercer wants to know the names of all the teenagers who walk so they can have a curfew. She's taken photographs of them from her porch. Buster Johnson truly believes people will be inclined to buy his gasoline if they are already stopped, rather than driving out a half mile to Stuart's. Stuart has four pumps. Four. Buster has one. Barton thinks the paving is for him.

Stuart's. It used to be a livery. Liveries all the way to California. No more. Enos Jafferty on Front Street, still. But his son's put in a pump. There had been more than a few liveries between Homer and Niagara, but that was then. She tastes a bit of bile. Nothing near as bad as on the Old Seneca Turnpike running along the canal. She records another dozen or more. Slash slash slash slash. The sun continues warm on her shoulders.

"Coming Saturday: *Hard to Handle*." Komár's problem was that he put *Ektase* on the marquee. *Das blaue Licht*. Teddy Lang turns toward the rise in his squad car and gives her a tentative, apologetic wave. She decides against counting him. He's out of sight before his tires meet the tracks. He should be sorry.

*

A woman with a stroller enters Federated. Colleen thinks she can hear the baby crying. She pauses. Mistaken. A crow.

Six or seven teenagers turn the corner onto Pleasant, to walk a quarter of a mile to Hudson's Apothecary, for his soda fountain and magazines. The high school is two blocks further on. Colleen can't tell if Marlene wants their business. She won't put a Coca Cola sign in her window. The cola man had offered her five dollars a month for the space. She'd turned it down. Turned him down. As he swigged from a bottle, face to the sky, chicken-necked, he'd swaggered. Hinted she'd lose her carbonation. Her "bubbly countenance," was the way he'd put it, neck sagging, face already to the kitchen, the back exit, the alley, his truck. Colleen wonders if the soda truck is a smooth ride. All of those bottles shaking and ready to explode. The carbon tanks. Fizz everywhere. The corners of her mouth twitch skyward. Soda jerk.

Yesterday, during lunch, Colleen'd walked down to Woolworths to pick up a spool of thread. She'd imagined Lady sitting on the bench facing the Grain and Feed, Lady's bench, a small heft of bread and a wedge of lettuce, waxed paper laying across her lap. Inside, Colleen'd browsed the hair dyes and turned down the aisle stocked with baby clothes. Swaddlings. She'd lingered. She'd given all of Robbie's away before the war. She can't remember who took them.

A young man appears from beneath the marquee, surprising only that he is on foot and doesn't "belong," as Grambly would say, "moving too fast." He catches her eye, and turns onto Pine toward the library. Grambly belongs. Stood so long at the corner once that a dog sniffed up and down his leg, sat, licked itself, stood, sniffed again, lifted its leg, and peed on him. Colleen surprises herself with a titter, hand to her mouth. Followed by a twinge. The light turns green and a half-dozen or more take a right turn toward the rise. Ford, Olds, Ford, Ford, Maxwell, Plymouth. It's surprising how many people do want to walk. "Nobody wants to walk anymore," puffs Grambly. Meaning he doesn't. Three hundred pounds oozing sweat. Just taking a step sets it to streaming down his face. *He* doesn't want to walk. *He* doesn't want to ride the ruts. One of the reasons he wants the road paved. One of the reasons he wants a new road.

"Excuse me ma'am." The young man has his hand out, offering her an ice from Spinelli's. Mint. He's filthy with road dust. His palm leaves its mark on the paper as she takes the ice. Thanks him. He has a French accent within a vowel or two of Mimi's. Face like a crow. Thin. Thinner than William's. Probably never breaks a sweat. She flirts with being annoyed—never been ma'am-ed before.

A Grand Marquis. Two more Fords. Roser down in Rome is doing well.

He has an ice of his own. She offers him the empty half of the bench, but he declines. His legs will cramp.

He nods at her pad. Guesses what she's about.

"You might as well count me." He slurps at the ice, already melting. "My feet raise dust as much as any REO." He looks to his pants, below the knees, slaps, and releases a small cloud. "Give me dirt roads every day."

Colleen blinks.

"Love country roads." Cloud settling. "Walking the ruts, finest thing in the world. High-wire act."

He's twitching. Ice gone, himself ready to follow. He melts away and over the rise. Suddenly, the entire town looks like it is caught in a photograph. The last time Colleen walked a rut, she was early on with Robbie. She'd twisted her knee and could barely walk for two weeks. All because William'd misjudged his tank.

Colleen can't keep up with her own ice and has to set it on the ground. She feels suddenly alone and twists against her stitch to the fountain and the rest of the square. Kenna and Sairy, mothers and their children, have vanished. She looks quickly to the sky for a hawk. Force of habit.

William had only ever misjudged one other time. On the way to Niagara. William Jr. pressing hard. William angry for having to think about it. Angry for having to stop. Angry for having to go. Drove right through Cards Corners or Wellington Center without thinking to check. Later, near Geneva, he'd nearly overheated the Limited with the hills. With the cumbrances, he might have said. Or already been thinking. Fortunately, he'd had several bottles of castor. Petroleum wasn't smooth enough for the Limited. They could have used that heat. It had been cold. Dark by the time they made Geneva, but he'd wanted to press on to Avon. If it hadn't been for Seneca Falls, they'd have been there by dark. Strangest of days. William had been racing a train when they were suddenly passed by a duck. It'd come up from a small pond as they passed, flew close, and then went right on by.

Colleen can't remember why she'd never said anything one way or another until it was too late. It wasn't because of Lorraine. Or Molly.

She stands. Stretches her back as best she can. Notes the Nash that rolls through the yellow. The Buick behind it rolling through the red as if being towed. Sits and slashes twice. Adjusts her pillow against another twinge. Taste of bile. Twelve hours was too much even then.

The farms along the canal, along the turnpike, had such fields they could barely see to the other side. The barns were French, one of the vendors had told them. That and Dutch. Mormons, said another. Angles in the wrong places. Windows in the wrong places, some like church windows. Not enough room for all the hay they might need, at least not so Colleen'd thought. It had been apple season and every vendor had a different kind. Roasted potatoes. Hot pork sausages flavored with fennel. Cheeses different from the cheese in Homer. Soft cheese. Wine enough to fill a radiator. One'd told William that it was cheaper than water. Better than water. William'd agreed. Too much water, he'd said. Bridges and ferries every other mile. The vendor'd grown angry. He'd owned a ferry. Lost it in July when the town finished a bridge. Put him out business. It was either vending or picking grapes like the Italians that passed through. Colleen had grimaced with William Jr. pressing against her bladder. She thinks to her bladder now, to the theater across the street, to the Falls. Robbie'd never pressed. Baby girl. Ghost child.

They'd arrived. The Falls. William had wanted to go over. Not over the falls, but over the bridge to the other side. To Canada. His family, way back, had smuggled the islands across to Canada. He'd never been. He'd later tell it that a woman went over just as they were driving the bridge. He liked to say that they could see the woman swirling. But she'd jumped a week earlier. For love, proclaimed the Canadian paper. Whispered the desk clerk at the Clifton House, sweating from the heatwave. As they'd driven the bridge, foot patrols stopped pedestrians, peeked under parasols.

After the ceremony—dinner and *Tillie's Punctured Romance*. The Falls and back? Felt like Officer 444 careening through all of creation. Like Chaplin. Or Lloyd.

She's still not entirely certain it was legal.

She can't sit. Stands. Paces. Minces across the street to the theater and inside. Her skirt's too tight at the knees.

*

Colleen emerges to a Model 47. Engine powerful enough to plough through drifts in winter. Heavy. Buddy Rooke buried one up to his axles out on County Road 15. Had to have Johnny Taggot pull him out with his tractor. Johnny told the story in Marlene's. Came in stomping the cold off himself. Said right off that he was surprised when he saw two girls inside. "Probably retarded," he'd said, cup of hot milk in his hands, "the way they laughed when I saw them. Not a French word, 'retarded.' Sounds like it though, like they tarred the road again. Probably came from Hoofdorp, all dressed in white the way they were." He was about to guess why they were in the 47, but the entire counter hushed him.

Colleen hurries back across the street to the square. The light favors Main Street. Long waits for Pine and Pleasant. Before the war, Karl stood in the middle of the intersection directing traffic—horses, bicycles, automobiles in a jumble. Pedestrians walking wherever they wanted. After the war, an electric light. She wonders, briefly, how long it will be before there is an electric counter. Slash. Her bladder still squeezed.

The 47 is clean. Whitewalls still white. A shine—it hasn't been on a country road recently, if ever. No rust. Can't be from Homer. Buddy Rooke's has a broken headlight where a baseball hit it. Parked it close to the ball field so everyone could see. This 47 isn't local. How he got here with his whitewalls still white is anybody's guess. Colleen unbuttons two more at the knees, adjusts her pillow again. Her back is pulling. She wonders how anyone can keep anything white anymore. The two girls in Buddy Rooke's 47 were probably ghosts. That's how people tell ghosts from the living—their clothes are clean, white. They've escaped the dirt of the world. Colleen pauses in the middle of a slash. She thinks she might be seeing a ghost car. She wonders whether ghost cars can carry a dent. Her mind idles. Wonders if ghosts can have tousled hair? If they can feel the scream? That would explain…or not, she thinks. The living can be ghosts.

Komár's first sheet wasn't all that white, but white didn't matter as much as still did. The rippling with the breeze made it difficult enough to see, so the dinge wasn't the problem Colleen'd've thought it'd've been. Seemed like a good idea at the time. Sitting outside watching *White Zombie* and *King Kong*. Bela Lugosi kissing the ghost of a girl in a casket. Officer 444 careening about the town. The bugs were something terrible.

William preferred to be moving. When he did stop to park, he preferred places like Settlement Road. Near the smaller of the cemeteries. Colleen'd wanted to get out, to see who they were visiting, who was keeping company while they kissed, but William wouldn't, they weren't *going* anywhere. The only reason he'd driven the Settlement Road was because no one else did. No ruts.

*

Sun. Glare off the bank's windows. She shades her eyes to see who is driving the Dodge, the De Soto, the Plymouth. Flickering with the sun. Flickering glint off the driver's-side windows would have given Velda a seizure. Slash slash slash. Her felt hat is already growing warm, brimless or nearly so, she takes it off, letting her hair loose. She wishes she could have finger waves, but her hair won't hold them. The Hudson, slash, has to be the reporter from Rome. The Hudson has to be borrowed. The sun feels good on her shoulders. Sleeveless blouse with buttons. A seemingly endless number of tiny buttons. Lady'd thought it looked lovely on her. Matching skirt, if only for the matching buttons continuing down the front. Lady'd thought it looked daring. Gray buttons against a white blouse. Gray buttons continuing down a black skirt. Pulling her knees together.

A Ford coming over the tracks backfires, exhaust spewing blue as it slows to the intersection. New Jersey plate. White on red. Hollis had been stepping into the street, but ducked with the backfire. The cloud masks the glare off the glass.

The reporter working the Zero Murder. Snoops something. Colleen still can't believe Zero's motorcycle simply exploded. She can't believe Snoops hasn't rallied Grambly and the Ladies Auxiliary over Zero's unborn. Goose's unborn. Vivian's unborn. Colleen settles on Miss Muldain. Miss Muldain's unborn. Between the *Legion* and *The Ode*, it appears she has a number of "aliases," as Snoops calls them. Perhaps Grambly *is* involved, sensing a conspiracy. No doubt he suspects Halloway. Colleen thinks she hasn't seen a Hoving ride through since the Naughts rode with the Belles through town on their way to the cemetery. Snoops disappears. Colleen has to laugh. He's being followed by Duds in a Packard. Borrowed as well. There's no money in news. She slashes him twice. Once for himself. Once for his stealing Snoops's by-lines. The Packard has been at the drive-in every Saturday, parked behind the bunker without a clear line of sight. Komár is ready to run him off the lot, but Duds's money is good. What he's doing in the car is a mystery.

Two weeks after Faye Wray wavered on screen, Komár decided to use a parachute. Colleen doesn't know where he found one. She is sure he hadn't jumped in the war. She isn't sure he was in the war. He drives a Model 50 now. That's why he strung up a sheet, then a parachute, and then put the wood backing to it, because he loves that 50. So much that he doesn't drive it. Doesn't want it to get dirty. The seats are white, of all things. He just wants to sit in it. Smell the insides. Doesn't want anyone else in it at all. Afraid they'll bring in the dirt.

Colleen begins to doubt that Komár is actually driving to Rome. He creeps along at a crawl, afraid to raise the dust. Even then, five miles seems to be all that he can endure. Five miles? The first week of May they'd "driven out." It'd been hot, hot as today, over eighty, sunshine. The evening had held the heat. Hot for so early. They'd driven out after the evening feature—*Daring Daughters*—a god-awful movie. Marian Marsh at her worst. They'd driven two miles, as far as the drive-in. The posts were in, waiting for the wires to be strung for the telephones. He'd brought a blanket. The ground was too wet, so he'd covered the seat with it. Afterwards, he'd retired the blanket to the closet off the projection room in the American. The 50 was too precious. To be honest, Colleen thinks, the 50 is ordinary as ordinary is.

She sets the pencil down. Hand to her stomach. Rests it there. She feels tired, whole body tired. She thinks to minerals. Dr. Lawell had her take Angostura bitters when she was pregnant with Des. He'd thought she'd been suffering stomach upset. Dr. Bearden, in his radio show from Rome, said that the bitters worked wonders, especially for women "suffering nerves, constipation, and various venereal diseases and other female complaints." "Like being pregnant," Hadley'd snarled. Musil refuses to carry bitters. Refuses Bonnare's Bathing Fluid. He'd said it was flimflam after seeing Bearden at the fair in Rome, bitters in one hand, Bonnare's in the other.

It had been a relief to see Desiré.

That first weekend, Komár used telephones. It was strange to be sitting in the car watching Wynne Gibson and Ginger Rogers in the middle of a field with the glow of the sun setting and the stars coming up behind. Even stranger to be hearing Ginger Rogers through the telephone, as if she were making a person-to-person call. Colleen thinks he put the telephone at the other end up against the projector's speaker. He couldn't have been using HT&T, running it through the telephone girls. It took him a couple of weeks to replace the telephones with speakers and build little boxes on the poles for them to set. Had to roll down the window to hear it. Colleen was surprised he hadn't thought of that first, what with Woolworths playing music in the street every day for years. Then there were the bugs…again. The whole car would be singing with the mosquitoes. Loud enough to overpower the speaker. So Komár tinkered… again. More wire and drivers could put the speaker in the car. Rest it right on the dash. He set them up like that to see how they would work. One of the Rischel boys forgot to put the speaker back at the end of the movie. Ripped it right off the pole when he drove off. Komár didn't know until the next night when someone parked next to the pole and found it missing.

Forty telephones opening night. There had been fifty cars. Ten cars had to pretend they were watching silent movies, but no one complained. A ballplayer from Rome took Robbie. Dodge Sedan. Colleen never asked if they had one of the telephones. Or maybe it was Robbie and the girls that opening night? Colleen had been in the bunker, the small cinder block projection building. It had been a warm night. Officer 444 careening, always careening, across the screen. *King Kong*. Faye Ray in white. Zombies. Girls screaming in parked cars.

Komár finally settled on radio broadcasts. It was obvious who went to the drive-in to watch the movies, and who didn't, by whether or not the cars had radios. Danny Barton can't be trusted even with the car of the week. Robbie mentioned the Delco in the ballplayer's Dodge "broke" after the first feature. They'd had to watch the movie as if it was silent. She said they'd made-up the dialogue as the movie went along. Sometimes the frequency Komár was using was overrun by WFIZ. Cagney would be flashing his eyes, pounding his fist, and screaming, when suddenly The Boswell Sisters were singing "Nothing is Sweeter Than You." Or in Hitchcock's movie when Helen Haye is about to blackmail Edmund Gwenn, Zona Gale's neighbors stole the dialogue. Robbie wears pants to the drive-in.

Komár has new plans for the American, though Colleen isn't sure exactly what they are. He has talked about morning showings for the men on the third shift. He has talked about showing old, old movies from before the war. She and Charlotte had been to Rome back before William. They'd seen some of the old old movies. *Twilight of a Woman's Soul. Tess of the Storm Country. Traffic in Souls.* Charlotte claimed that Colleen'd stolen William. But she hadn't. William had only ridden out with Charlotte in the front seat once.

A Bugatti comes over the rise, the tracks, a slow glide to the red. Colleen is surprised Grambly & Co. allow one in town. It's a surprise they let Komár own the theater. They'd run Carmine Valentino out. He'd been transferring

35mm films to 16mm, and they arrested him, but they never found the copies. They'd claimed he was Rudolph's brother and that he had an entire closet filled with sheiks. Mostly, it was because he was Italian and made the ladies clutch themselves as they passed, shy, giggling. "Bella Donna," he'd say, with a sweeping smile. One after another. "Bella Donna." They'd run him out. No evidence. The closet had been empty too, or so say the rumors. The Bella Donnas all smiles. Or so say the rumors. He packed off to Florida. Two, three years off the tax roll and they sold it to Komár for next to nothing.

Colleen's startled. Someone is humming "Nothing is Sweeter than You."

Komár's been slipping those 16mms into his schedule. Most everything he had coming from Germany were 16mm. He keeps the 16mm projector tucked away in the small room behind the closet, but Sunday, with *Das blaue Licht* and *Ektase*, it was the 35mm tucked away in the closet. Teddy should be run out of town. Him and Karl. Grambly & Co. as well. Pile them into a couple of Bugattis and send them straight up to Collins Landing.

Patrick had taken her to see *Bella Donna*, sneaking her in at the last moment so no one would see them there. This was after her summer at The Hollow. She'd come back so pale her mother had put her to bed. Nothing at Musil's would have helped her eyes, dark and darker, like Pola Negri's. Desiré had found a family in Moselle who would take him. William Jr. had done something on the farm, fencing the pigs perhaps, and was proud to show it off, dragging her out of the black sedan and through the mud to see a saddleback before her mother threw a shawl over her shoulders and helped her inside. He'd named it Chloë. Robbie had hugged her and told her not to die. Colleen thinks Patrick had taken her to *Way Down East*, but he couldn't have known.

Komár says he's planning to show a Pola Negri next weekend. He has several, but he says he's going to make it a surprise. Colleen's certain it will be, hopes it will be the one where she washes herself with snow. Colleen welcomes the goose bumps and the chill and feels her nipples as they swell, ache a phantom ache, too soon, too soon for Charlotte's nipple tape, too soon to worry about secrets. Negri is hilarious pouring perfume all over herself, her hair, down her blouse. And the man looking at his keister in a hand mirror. Colleen breaks a smile. Patrick hadn't understood. As much as she'd wished him to, Patrick hadn't understood most things.

A Phaeton. To hear Hollis tell it, it's a creamy ride. Creamy de-*luxe*. Takes the bump out of the ruts. Colleen, slashing, isn't so sure. She is sure that

Lloyd called Charlotte "creamy de-luxe" once upon a time, and not because she didn't have the bump. He hadn't known Colleen was sitting near the back in Malley's when he'd come in. Malley's had places like that, places people could sit, behind a pole, just out of sight and left to themselves. Ace Crawford kept the name but took the poles out when he bought restaurant.

Lloyd had been sitting at the counter. Colleen could see the street from where she had been sitting, table against the window, see the cemetery, what had been the cemetery before they'd taken the bodies to outer Main and planted the chestnuts. At the time, the headstones were black from a fungus, so black the names were unreadable. The town had debated whether or not to wirebrush the fungus. The bristles had taken names as well. Turned them into new stones for the next generation. Nothing to read either way. Colleen can't remember who, but Rooke or Nott or Planck wanted to move all of the bodies out past the new gasoline station, said people liked their dead out of sight. Or, maybe they just wanted to move the stones, leave the dead where they lay, out of sight. Colleen can't recall whether or not the bodies were moved. There had been a summer filled with digging. Full with holes. After the war. She shudders and shakes away the thought that there could be a body buried under the bench. Feet sneaking out from under toward the bank. Head to the church behind her.

Lloyd had been sitting at the counter talking about his Nash Special and Charlotte and driving back roads to Rome, as if anyone didn't know what he meant. Colleen wouldn't know about Charlotte being creamy de-luxe. She had always been on the up, until The Blow, drifts ten feet at the farm, higher in The Settlement. Lloyd had been talking big to Frank. Zoë'd come out from the kitchen smelling of cloves and cumin. She'd heard Lloyd and slapped his plate on the counter, sending a sausage sliding off onto his pants. He'd jumped with the grease and yelped a "what the" and Colleen started laughing and Lloyd suddenly knew she was there, and he was rubbing the front of his pants with a napkin, but it was only making it worse. He stopped as the Dank boys came in and Freddy said "Hey, Lloyd, taking care of yourself now?" and Zoë came around to the front of the counter and picked the sausage up off the floor and asked if he was done with it or if he needed a little more time. Colleen can't even see a Special without it sending her. Charlotte later heard what Lloyd'd said, and she hadn't cared. Said she *was* creamy de-luxe and it was about time the world knew it. Colleen doesn't think Charlotte knew what Lloyd meant. In another world Charlotte might have been retarded. Or maybe she was only pretending to be retarded. She was always feigning something. She sent a postcard to Gerald Woosier, one from a folding camera, with her with a pillow up her dress. Scared Gerald to death. Not that he didn't deserve it. It's much harder to pretend the pillow isn't there. Wearing a sackcloth, complaining of the troubles to avoid....

Colleen pauses with a flush of heat. She has that wrong. The dates. The Blow. Lloyd. Charlotte. William. Flash of sun against Volker's Pontiac 6, yellow spokes dizzying as they spin. Colleen blinks, consciously. Velda had her first seizure in it five or six years ago, after the birth of her daughter. It'd taken how many seizures before Volker convinced her to go to Syracuse? Bromide. Musil carried it, only for her, and scoffed at her doctor in Syracuse, saying there had to be something better. He'd been tempted to make something of his own. "Everything is chemistry," he'd said to the police when they'd asked him about explosives and the Zero murder. All of that in a flash of sun, in a blink, in the quarter spin of a yellow spoke. Could the chemistry teacher have done it? Blown up the Zero? Colleen recalls William's grandmother reporting that *her* mother had a seizure when she was born. Robbie's great-great-grandmother. That her doctor had told her mother that it happened all the time during childbirth. Colleen is thankful it hasn't happened to her. Holds her stomach and closes her eyes against the next one two three cars flashing as they pass. Slash slash slash. Thinks to Des. Hardest of the three. She still blesses The Hollow. Had she remained in town, Dr. Lawell could have killed her with his scalpels. "Never met a knife he didn't like," says Hadley.

Flash of insight. Zero was the Rome connection with the birth control league. She'd have been too young when Dr. Cooper lectured. Colleen and Hadley and Cosette had been on their way when a winter storm closed the road. "God's will!" from the *Legion*. "God's will!" from the *Legion* when Cooper died two years ago. And with the explosion, "God's will." Colleen feels her heart skip. Nervous. The *Legion* reporter? Snoopy Fane or something.... Snooping around Lady and Clara and Kay as well.

Flash of doubt. Lady wasn't in the league? She couldn't have been. Could she?

Colleen's head spins. Kay teaching in the Homer school. Zero in Rome. Lady working Woolworths?

Volker Jörn in a baby blue Oldsmobile. Colleen clears her head. She wonders when he came over.

*

Three small girls in slickers follow their mother past the bank. Rischel had called for rain. The sun already burns the back of Colleen's neck. Clear sky and hot. Even now, Colleen twisting to see the clock. Volker's gone, down Main and over the bridge. The three little ducks cross Pleasant, arms out, flapping their wings.

Viktor's Pierce Arrow. Pierce Arrows. Once, one of the most expensive cars. But the 81 is a cheap model. Not like the 36 that John Planck was driving several of months ago. Shame he kissed a tree with it. Gold interior and a dual six. The way everything tilts makes it look fast standing still. John used to sit at the light with his arm hanging out the window, waiting for the green. Then he'd sit for all to see until someone behind him started on his horn. Said he thought he *was* moving. He'd say it with a sly smile and a flash of gray in his eyes. He was going to get a straight eight, even talked big about a straight twelve. He couldn't have handled that much speed. He probably hit the tree going twenty but thinking he was doing eighty. Hadley said it was just a twisted frame. Eighty would have cut that car in half. Colleen thinks maybe Planck was just sitting there waiting for Mimi to notice him. Flashing his eyes like Valentino. Expected him to walk up and kiss the glass until the James kid started sniffing around. Dogs. Expected *him* to lift a leg and pee on the glass what with all of his carryings on. Can't blame them. Mimi has *it*. Could be a regular "It" girl if she'd ever get out of town. Strange boy. Came back from college with grease in his hair, holding it straight up in the front like he'd been scared out of his mind. Mimi has *it*. If she was mine, thinks Colleen, I'd buy her a ticket straight to Hollywood. Feels a twinge of guilt over Robbie. Even so, one has to wonder. Mimi's got the smiles for the boys, but…. Colleen brushes away a ladybug. Grambly plans to have the James boy on the shovel for the rest of the summer. Moving a cemetery with Tuber Nott. They deserve each other, thinks Colleen. And Robbie deserves a ticket straight to Hollywood as well. Colleen can see her baby girl's name on the marquee, the town preening over it, over her. Robbie Pierce in…. Of course she'll change her name. Robbie O'Shea in…. Her grandfather would approve. It's not as though William ever knew.

Robbie and Mimi had been sitting in their usual seats, eight back and dead center, Sunday, when Teddy and Karl smashed their way in. Karl, in his lunge for Komár, knocked the projector over. Teddy yanked at the moving reels, pulling 16mm celluloid in whirls across the floor. The struggle between Karl and Komár had their feet scuffled and tangled in the film, breaking the strips, heels ground into the crouching Hedy Kiesler. Teddy took the second reel, the one sitting on the table next to the projector, and flung it through the projection window. Teddy could have been in the movies. The evil eye he cast as he turned back, black and white, piano rising, every villain's dream—the destruction of his very own world.

The evil eye all of a sudden shocked at the sight of Colleen, the recognition that she was there in the booth, evil turned, exorcised. Teddy suddenly sheepish then quickly buried in the officious.

Below, under the balcony—utter silence.

Robbie and Mimi, all alone and exposed near the front, saw the reel flying toward them, film trailing, twisting, caught in slow motion, in the collective inhale of thirty sets of lungs. Karl had Komár in cuffs and, with Teddy, was pushing him down the stairs. Thirty sets of eyes caught in a collective blink. Komár was yelling something in German or French or Hungarian or some other unspeakable. Untranslatable.

Robbie and Mimi raced the rows gathering the film.

Cosette appeared in the projection room, shrugged a "who knows what Komár is screaming" and, with her appearance and the shrug, was already bringing a smile to Colleen's worry. She began helping Colleen gather all of the strips of film, then all of the cans from the store room. It took half a dozen trips to slip everything into the alley and inside Marlene's, worrying all the while that Karl and Teddy might be back. The projector was destroyed. The films, but for *Ektase*, were safe.

Marlene started a fresh pot of Sanka for Cosette. Colas for Robbie and Mimi. Colleen collapsed in the booth across from the cash register.

"I don't want to know," said Marlene, with "tell me later" in her eyes.

One or two, then three, four, five of the "women beneath the balcony" slipped in, eyes still in shock. Their feet snuck them along, exposed to the mirror running the length of the counter, took them to the booths in the back where they could sort it through, out of sight, without the glare of sun as it reflected off the glass HT&T. Another trickle of women filling Marlene's, booths, tables, counter. Whispers. Marlene turns on the radio. The switchboard in the window across the street was already ablaze with gossip.

Colleen's smile spreads, sloping ear-ward with the memory, and she applauds, a slow clapping, pencil dropping, intersection from red to green, red and green at the same time from where she sits. Her smile pops into an aborted guffaw.

Komár. Arrested, but not charged, and so, released, with a reprimand from the Chief of Police. Komár hadn't been able to decide whether or not to tell the Chief that his wife was in the audience, tucked up under the balcony. Perhaps the Chief already knew. Marlene would have confirmed—a lemon fizz and an oatmeal cookie that left an oily stain on her gloves. If Grambly'd had a wife, she'd have been there as well. If Grambly'd had a wife, she'd have had a flask. She'd have had veronal.

Komár. Released. Marlene said he'd stopped for dinner on his way home. The theater remained dark. She'd told him that Colleen had the films. That the projector had been destroyed.

Marlene's. Komár had first come into Marlene's in December, just after he'd bought the theater, face covered with sawdust. He'd asked Marlene for a "fitz," or so it sounded, and had lost his words at the sight of Colleen.

Colleen smiles at the "fitz," runs her hand over her stomach, watches two young boys with bats and gloves chase each other across Main, into the square and off behind her, past the church and beyond, to the park beside the seventh street cemetery. Slashes a few more cars. Fords, mostly. Hester Wade with a lime green pillbox hat. Lime. The new mauve. Powdering her nose at the red.

Colleen isn't used to stopping words.

A "fitz." His mustache filtering the bubbles. The mustache caught her. She couldn't look away, wondering, but not sure what to wonder. Her father and half the town had sported mustaches way back, heavy. Stooped over with the weight of them. She sniggers. Then, hand to her upper lip, feels for the baby fines of her own. One of her uncles had clean cheeks, but a mustache that covered his chin. Never married. All of them thinking to Roosevelt. Rough and tough Teddy. All of them happy to be rough and tough themselves, until he pushed the blue line.

"A mercy," her grandfather had said, that the line was drawn where it was. "It's nice to put a shovel in the ground without the government come snooping. Without the "forever wild." Robber barons lining up for mineral rights and Roosevelt's planting trees." More words in the space of a minute than he utters in a day. Unless he's talking potatoes. He'd inhaled for another speechifying, this one directed at the WPA and 750 acres. But had grown distracted by a small patch of late blight.

Colleen sniggers. William had been baby smooth. Colleen suspected he polished his face as much as he polished the Limited. Patrick? Hair too thin, never had the choice of a mustache, let alone a beard. Now Komár with his "fitz" and his speechless and his invitation to the construction as he tore old columns out from under the balcony, tore out the stage. Colleen remembers thinking how many productions she'd taken Robbie to after the war. *The Little King*. One about a dumb wife or a dumb cake. One by a German, *Literature*, she thinks, surprised that she remembers. Or maybe it was *Letters*. Dana Brooks had wanted her to audition. "You have just the thing," he'd said, emphasizing *thing* like it was something other than what people thought it was. "And thin like Clara Bow." But her hair couldn't hold a curl then. Later, perhaps, he might have convinced her. After the bob. After Louise Brooks. She resists touching her hair. Resists making the mental note of looking at dyes in Musil's. Again. Slash.

Monday morning. Rain. No good for Grambly, who was livid over the delay. Worse for Hollis, who hadn't a clue. Colleen arrived at work and was given a half-day. No counting on Monday.

Half day. Half pay.

On her way home, she'd paused to chat with Marlene, who told her Komár had been released. Of course Colleen had already heard. She stopped at Finnegan's. He had fresh cabbage from The Settlement. She decided, on a whim, to see if Gunther still had a bit of brined brisket. Gunther brines with juniper berries. The butcher had.

Then, home. The stairs and the kitchen. The walls the same awful green.

She'd sat. Just sat. Listening to the radio. At a loss.

Watching the rain against the window. At a loss.

The sound of Robbie's feet on the steps, ghost child followed by a second, by Mimi's, and the open and shut of the door and the "Can Mimi stay for dinner?" Robbie's smile had been infectious. Mimi "glowing" with the humidity.

Colleen'd set Mimi to work on the potatoes.

"Peel twice as many as you think," she'd said, thinking to William Jr.

Robbie'd spun the dial on the radio on the off chance that a new station would suddenly be there. Something from Chicago? Or further west? Sometimes Robbie is shy about saying "Hollywood" out loud. She hadn't mentioned it in a month. Colleen wondered, again, why she hadn't mentioned Mare's Nest.

Colleen wonders, with the slightest of a breeze whiffling her hair, why she hasn't mentioned Mare's Nest. Twists on the bench as far as the stab in her ribs will allow to see how close to noon it is.

Just past ten. Feels later with the sun growing stronger on her shoulders. She slashes ten times in anticipation of the church's toll. An eleventh. And a twelfth in anticipation of lunch. She should have brought something besides her lunch, besides the egg sandwich. Something to nibble as she sits.

Brisket and cabbage. Her grandmother's recipe. For the loss. For the soul. She'd gathered herself. Taken the brisket and the butter from the ice box. Rifled the back of the cabinet housing the large pot for the small bag of juniper berries. Gunther brines with juniper berries. Not nearly enough.

Her own mother had forsaken the juniper even before Grambly and his minions made it illegal, complaining about stomach cramps and light-headedness even from eating pork sausage. Mimi'd helped with the potatoes and mustard while Robbie ran next door for a clove. Cloves. Bay leaf. Pepper. Allspice. Colleen's grandmother made sure Colleen always had a little juniper.

But for the company of Robbie and Mimi, she'd have wished she'd been at The Hollow, with Desiré and the rest, for they'd always found their way to the "railroad room" off the basement and returned with a bottle of wine. Not wine from the lakes, she thinks, with muted apologies to Zero, but wine from Italy or France or Spain. Once, from Washington State smuggled down from Canada. William would have been proud.

The Hollow. With Desiré and the rest.

She brushes Saturday away as if a mosquito. It returns just as quickly.

They'd eaten over small talk. The can factory. The falls. Hollywood. Greta Garbo and John Barrymore. Afterward, while the girls cleaned up, Colleen went to the back, to the closet, and pulled out a suitcase. She'd emptied it on the table. Two reels and over two-thousand feet of film. Brittle. Broken. Tangled. Creased. *Ektase.*

They'd worked for hours. The girls puzzling the strips, Colleen taping them together with Komár's splicer. Colleen'd been reminded of Ma Pierce's quilting bees, six women gossiping over fox and geese and broken dishes. Colleen had been invited, but too proud, too modern then, too fast to sit still for more than a few minutes. By the time she'd grown to know her mother-in-law, taking William Jr. and Robbie to see their grandmother, William off in Mare's Nest, remarried, to Charlotte, Ma Pierce had given up the quilts. The gossip. It never had amounted to much, she'd said later about who'd said what to whom. Grambly running with Netty Hayes. Storey Lincoln stealing $200 from the library. The sort of gossip followed by an "ooh" and a pricked finger.

"This is hard," said Robbie. "There are too many horses."

Colleen had been bent close to the splicer. "Horses?"

"I can't tell them apart."

Mimi'd laughed. "Some are statues."

"But they're all black!"

Colleen leans back against the pillow. She had never really thought that Robbie was so full with melodrama. Wonders, idly, as a black Hudson rolls through a red light, how many horses would she have counted if she'd have had to have done this twenty years ago.

"Can *you* tell?" Robbie'd held two strips up for Mimi to look at.

"That one has a saddle." Mimi's crooked tooth visible between her fingers as she tried to hide her giggle, saving Robbie from certain embarrassment. Mimi's fingers were delicate, her nails polished, but without color.

"It'd be easier if they were motorcycles."

Colleen doubts there would have been as many. Horses. Wagons. Carriages. Even so, people hadn't moved about as much. The Hudson returns, whitewalls barely turning as the driver looks across the passenger seat through the window at her. She doesn't know him. The hair rises on the back of her neck. A man had done that in a Rockaway pulled by a bay twenty years earlier. It'd been a day like this day, warm, sunny, and she and Charlotte had been walking up from the river past Woolworths when he'd brought the horse's walk down to a shuffle. She'd felt Charlotte stiffen as he stroked his beard, his other hand on the reins. Charlotte hadn't know him. Neither had Colleen.

"Your grandfather was always angry that I couldn't tell the difference between a draft and a carriage horse."

"Potatoes, too," snickered Robbie. "He'd pound his fist on the table," and she'd pounded by way of an example, setting the splicer to wiggling, "and say 'Chenango!' of what the grocer sold."

Colleen'd laughed. "I bought a Chenango once. Just to set him to a rant."

"Gunther just received lemons," said Mimi. Mysteriously. "An hour ago."

Colleen'd made a note to remember to stop on her way home from work the next day. If he had any left. Perhaps on her way. They might as well set in her clutch as in his crates.

"What else have you heard?" Colleen had had her eye to the splicer, matching the film's sprocket holes to the tape's. She'd sensed Mimi didn't want to say.

"Aha!" said Robbie, matching stallion to mare.

Of course Mimi couldn't say what she'd heard through the switchboard, or, even, who was speaking with whom about what, but Robbie let it slip, in between horses.

Clara Shure hadn't killed Edwin.

Colleen knows that. Karl and Teddy know. Even Grambly knows. The poor girl was just lost, seeing her husband buried in corn when the silo collapsed at the Grain and Feed a year ago. Edwin had been first with the shovel.

Colleen is certain that Clara hadn't killed Lady, either.

Marlene hates quilting. Colleen is thinking about lunch. Nor is Marlene terribly fond of her brothers, William and Jemmy, who taunted her as she developed.

Of course Mimi couldn't say what she'd heard through the switchboard. She could say Grambly had strolled in and offered the girls free ice cream from Stacy's Ice House if they'd listen to Wilson's and Halloway's telephone calls. She could say that they all refused. Later that week, Halloway placed a call to Washington. Mimi was making the transfer when she heard a series of clicks. Wire-tapping, she'd said as she'd matched cloud to cloud. Wire-tapping. Every new girl is trained in etiquette and other things, including deciphering wire-tapping from other noise on the lines. She'd done what every new girl is trained to do. She pulled the jack. Disconnected before the call went through.

Grambly never strolled, thinks Colleen. He can't move that quickly.

"Never!" said Robbie.

"Cross my heart," said Mimi, inscribing an "x" with the same hand that pushed jacks. Pulled jacks.

Wire-tapping. Patrick had said they did it in the war. William's father wouldn't talk on a telephone for fear of being overheard. His speech stolen, he'd said when asked.

"I'll bet that's why the James boy...," Robbie'd said.

A shiver ran through Mimi's upper-back/shoulders. "He works for Hirem, not Grambly."

"Same thing," Robbie'd hissed. Angry. Nearly gelding the stallion.

Colleen nods to herself. Same thing. Like Hoover's thugs. Wondering how Robbie is so smart.

They'd worked in silence, fingers sliding celluloid about the table. A shell game, like the fair in Rome, the charlatans, the fortune tellers, pickpockets. The theater owner had rented a tent and was showing movies against the canvas, drumming up business for his matinées. He'd had to crank the projector by hand, and, so, a herky-jerky *Kidnapped in New York*, Baby Osborn whisked away by crooks. People appearing and disappearing with the cuts run through so fast it was like entire strips of film were altogether missing.

"I wonder how it turns out." Robbie looks to the other reels, mercifully intact.

They'd rescued her, of course. Colleen shifts again, and yet again on the bench. She's trying to find a comfort spot. Grambly passing behind the window, keeping his eye on her.

"In Tiche, probably," said Mimi. And, seemingly without any prompting, "My grandmother worked there. As a volunteer. She said the girls looked scared all of the time."

Colleen'd changed the subject. "They're starting to oil the roads. Done by the time the fair opens."

Robbie grew excited. "Will there be motorcycle races this year?"

"Hedy looks afraid." Mimi holds up a strip of fifteen or twenty frames. "She's beautiful."

The World's Fair, in May, in Chicago, had an incubator. Colleen slashes at the thought.

"There was a bi-plane giving rides for a dime back before you were born," Colleen'd leaned away from the splicer, away from the pain in her lower back. "It crashed the day after we left. The pilot died." She'd paused with the silence. "The next year there were bi-plane races."

"Cool!" Then, "Why do boys always talk about themselves?"

A patchwork before them in the growing dusk. Frame after frame of Hedy Kiesler, naked, stilled, and blurred, in that half-world, in that twilight, the soft edges of day and night, the moment between inhale and exhale, Robbie and Mimi's fingers sliding the frames about the table, medium shots and close-ups, saved by pans, stymied by jump cuts, some resolved by tracing scratches in the film, scratches that ran twenty or thirty frames.

Mimi held one strip to the incandescent, a close-up of Hedy Kiesler, upside down twists downside up, twists her own head to match Kiesler's, then turned to Colleen, and said, "Did you ever…?" and then silence, Mimi's easy familiarity stifled, black flecks meshing with the brown in Mimi's gray-blue, turning an spoken question mark into space…free floating, then gone with nothing of the opacity of Hedy Kiesler's flight. A two-step backtrack. Colleen didn't seem to notice, bent to the splicer as she was, splicing Kiesler, cowering, naked behind a fallen tree, splicing Kiesler to Aribert Mog, eyes searching, horse still, thinking she should have been wiping clean each strip before the splice. She double-checked the fit, the tape, and considered the possibility that the sprocket holes are more important than the images themselves.

Colleen didn't seem to notice, but she felt Robbie tighten. How could she not? Every heart beat, every movement, clenched fist, kick, twist, set off sparks in her womb.

"Did you ever...?" She imagines Vaughn De Leath crooning over a radio microphone. "Did you ever...?" she hums to no melody and finds herself lost in the pause.

*

Colleen emerges once again from the theater. Cosette sits on her bench, clearly waiting for her return. She offers a large smile when Colleen nears. A beautiful smile that showcases the shine in her front teeth. Patrick wasn't her fault. Colleen's grandfather had said "Bah!" Followed by something about her being French and how she should have been smarter than to take up with a Rooke. Colleen's mother had tsked. Colleen had bitten her tongue. Robbie had started to say something, but William Jr. had kicked her under the table.

Colleen is afraid to return the smile. Afraid to ask "What now?"

Cosette helps her with her pillow. She offers Colleen a different smile, one that knows. Colleen looks away, to the First National. Inhales.

"What now?"

They both know Colleen isn't talking about *Ektase*.

Cosette follows Colleen's eyes to the bank. Grambly's empire. It's been nearly a year since Cosette lost her home to Grambly. To "the scourge." To 1932. Grambly, in matters mortgages, doesn't need Westcroft's services. He doesn't want to "collect."

Colleen slashes. A dozen or more for the show of it. A dozen or more penciled slashes. The lead is dull from the morning's work, but sharp enough to puncture the paper.

Cosette is laughing at her performance. Laughing at Colleen.

"Hey, old lady," says Cosette, story at the ready. Twisted tooth, nearly matching Mimi's, for all to see.

"Hey yourself, old lady," says Colleen, one year to the day younger than her benchmate. September 7th. Three weeks out. They haven't decided how they'll be celebrating.

Two boys on roller skates roll past the bank and through the intersection against the light. They coast the decline toward the river and out of sight.

"The factory was condemned," says Colleen, explaining the padlocked doors. "That's the way Grambly does it."

"Condemned?" Mispronounced as innocently as she can behind a twisted tooth and thirty-six years. As innocently as she can behind her French accent.

Colleen smiles in spite of herself. Her own front teeth peeking through her lips. She knows what's coming. Cosette tells the best stories.

"Entendant, dans le village…," and she's back to English and on her way. A man, from the village, from before the war, a Frenchman who went off to Arabia or Africa, came back with syphilis. "Now that's 'condemned,'" she says, triumphantly.

Colleen groans. Cosette catches the source. Changes the subject to something lighter. Rumor, Lettie has hundreds of letters that she never sent. Her eyes sparkle.

"Entendant, dans le village…," smiling with the beauty of the day. She tells of two women in Frise, France who had grown old together, vieille célibataires, full with unrequited love. They passed, at breakfast one morning, across from each other at the table, arsenic, hands clenched in rigor. The German soldiers found them three days later as they went from house to house in search of a saboteur. A young private had opened the door to the attic, one that swung downward, and thousands upon thousands of letters cascaded, burying the soldat to the waist.

"They say," says Cosette, with the wisdom of the world, "the boy's poor girlfriend felt the rush from two hundred miles away, and, overwhelmed by the loosing of such love, felt her heart swell and swell until it burst. She, too, dead. A casualty of love."

Casualties, thinks Colleen. "And the boy?"

"He fled to America after the war. To escape his grief."

Their eyes follow a young couple around the corner. A pedestrian or two go by. Veblen Wells spits on the sidewalk outside the bank.

"He was so sad that after leaving Ellis Island he threw himself into the East River from the Hell Gate Bridge."

Love lost. Lost love. Colleen thinking back to Niagara Falls and the swirl of white described in the papers. "All that's left of love," intoned one. She imagines Vaughn De Leath crooning over a radio microphone. William had missed her 17th birthday, just two weeks before their mad dash to Niagara.

"Josephine Baker," says Cosette, as though she's read Colleen's mind. She probably has. "Josephine Baker," correcting her, "would have sung it wonderfully."

Colleen, able to read Cosette's mind as well, thinks Baker would have been singing it in Paris, after the Germans. Had it been written.

They aren't all bad, as two young girls skip past Hollis and toward the rise. In a minute, maybe less, they will be over the tracks and out of sight. A string of three cars flicker Colleen's view of them, frame and frame, out of sync, for a moment when the middle Ford accelerates, and she slashes in vengeance. Two young girls. Three automobiles.

"It wasn't all bad," says Cosette, shifting her weight, her skirt wrinkling against the bench.

Colleen thinks briefly to a hot iron, but Cosette brings her back. To the street and another three slashes, and, with the shift in weight, an inhale.

"Entendant, dans le village…"

Colleen feels as though a ghost kicked her in the stomach.

Cosette is saying something about Germans. German soldiers stripped and bathing naked in the Rhône, shelled churches and homes in the background, a baby snatched, a young French mother screaming "Aidez-moi! Mon bébé!" and a squad of naked Germans racing through the streets to catch the kidnapper.

Of course Cosette arrived in Homer with her baby, Patrice. Patrick had "done the right thing" by leaving Colleen for his French wife and their newborn. After Patrick's death, Cosette had renamed Patrice, Racine. Perhaps for spite. Colleen never asked. Maybe someday. Racine turned thirteen in June. Maybe twelve. Women can't count.

"Hundreds of letters never sent," Colleen says aloud. "Mon bébé!"

Several cars slow for the light.

Cosette leans close. "A scandal," mysteriously.

Colleen's eyebrow flutters upward. In the space of that flutter, recognition.

"Grambly."

A shoulder bump, Cosette leaning close, Colleen completes the bump.

Cosette adjusts her front. Colleen her hat. Flushes. Her fingers move toward her shoulder, ready to close on a strap.

But what? they think at the same time.

"What difference can it make?"

A scandal.

Colleen unbuttons another button.

A birthday present to themselves. A celebration.

A scandal.

"Water."

"Sewage."

"Bodies."

"Dead or alive?"

"Documents."

"Documents?"

"Documents."

"Documents."

Cosette tips her head onto Colleen's shoulder.

"What is Komár showing Sunday?"

"Anders als die Andern." Colleen is afraid for her pronunciation.

"Aren't we all?"

*

The church strikes noon. The town square clock points to six after. Colleen realizes she's drifted to Episcopalian time. The light turns red, green, red as she gathers her pencil, pad, and pillow. She bends to recover her hat from the grass. Her jacket. Feels a twinge, nearly a cramp. Hollis steps out of the bank, laceless shoes ashine. Checks his watch against the church. Straightens his vest. Steps over Veblen's spit. Turns the corner, walking two blocks down Pleasant to The Sullivan. Lunch. Cigars. And the amenities of the back room. Colleen follows her feet, across Pine Street and past the theater. Pine Street. Used to be called Park Street. Before that, Cemetery Street. Or so Clem Dinning'd said. She's avoiding The Sullivan, the men from the town building, the bank, the lawyer's offices, thick with smoke and the smell of vodka, even in the outer rooms where the ladies are recently allowed. Her feet carry her mind to Saturday. She'll borrow Hadley's Flying Cloud. Perhaps. Better if Hadley would drive her, if she has the time. Best if she would, just in case. The Flying Cloud doesn't handle the curves as well as she'd like; it would take too long to be back in time. Her feet carry her to Marlene's. The glass door swings shut behind her. It's crowded. She's engulfed by the smell of the grill, and her stomach rises, upward, two, three buttons. She swallows and again. Emma turns strips of bacon, making room for a dozen spiced sausages. Colleen's forgotten that Robbie isn't working today. Then remembers that Robbie and Mimi have driven up to the Falls. Then, the momentary thought that they were headed in the wrong direction when she saw them this morning in the Coupe headed Rome-ward.

Marlene compliments her for her blouse. She tells her she looks tired and apologizes for the smell of grease and fat. Onions. Milk. Offers a cup of coffee. Extra-fine grind. "Pressed." Colleen avoids looking across the counter to the mirror. She knows she's tired. She doesn't need to be reminded. Doesn't need to see the dark under her eyes. She slips the egg sandwich from her pocket, orders a cookie. Marlene looks the other way, to the door. Calls out to Dotty to stopper it open. "It's hot," she says. There's an "amen" from a couple of young men in the booth closest to the street as if they've rehearsed. The fresh air helps further settle Colleen's stomach.

"Are you going out to the farm? Or, should I say 'when?'" Colleen sees Marlene tighten, but Colleen's only being conversational.

Marlene plays with a Spud, with a match, almost strikes it before setting it down again beside the register.

The musk from the women at the counter competes with the lavender passing behind her. She buries her nose in her sandwich.

"'When I get a day," Marlene says. "I can't even get to a movie."

"I'm thinking about taking Robbie. She hasn't been in months." Colleen wishes it wouldn't be a surprise visit, that Ma Pierce had a telephone. Ma Pierce doesn't seem to mind the surprise. Seems to enjoy the company. Marlene is happy her mother doesn't have a telephone. She'd have to call. Once a week, at least. Jemmy can take care of her just as easily. Take care of the pigs. Jemmy and Bert. Marlene's never liked Bertie. Something to do with pies, thinks Colleen. At least that's what Marlene tells people busy enough to wonder.

"People have too much time," says Colleen, spotting Halloway as he drives past, driver's-side window flashing briefly with the sun, on down to the river. She stirs her coffee. Touches the sugar, but sets it aside.

Marlene's eyebrow arches. Today?

Colleen nods. "The man from Washington drove through an hour ago." A Ford, of course. VA plates, black on white.

The "A-mens" push their plates to the edge of the table. Dotty scurries up to clear them.

"Dessert?"

They decline. Rise. Pay Marlene at the register. One flips a dime to the table. It rolls to the vinegar, ketchup, salt, napkins…tails.

"She's welcome to a few days off."

"Komár has *Lawyer Man*, Joan Blondell, this weekend. I could take the register." Already forgetting Hadley's Flying Cloud, Ma Pierce, and pies.

"What's Grambly about this week?"

"Same as every week. Watching. Watching Halloway mostly."

"Hoovering. That's what Rischel would say."

Colleen slips the cookie into her purse. "The question is Hollis."

She browses the compacts in Musil's. The eyeliners. Bath salts. Blush. Buys a small tin of aspirin. Feels the acids in her stomach.

The sun is hard against the glass of HT&T, so hard Colleen can barely read the letters, let alone see who's in the window. She almost prefers it boarded. She is a little surprised the James boy isn't still in jail or facing a fine. She can only suppose that Grambly needs him in the sewer more that he needs the boy in jail. Or that he doesn't like the owner of HT&T. No one knows who that might be. Greer Tennant hires the girls and sets them up in the window. Hemlines must be in the contract. Colleen shades her eyes, wishes she could shade her ears as the town paddy races up from the river and through the red light, Karl Harring hanging out the window yelling and trying to wave cars away. A De Soto nearly broadsides the wagon. The wagon nearly rolls over, Harring is tossed into the street. The back door opens and an uncountable number of McMahons and Danks tumble out and around the corner. Should be the Rischels, especially so, given their antics last summer. Colleen shades her eyes again. Blinks. The wagon is already over the rise, Keystone Cops passing with the heat.

She leans forward, looking down Main, down two blocks toward the river. She can still see Lady, on the bench, eating her lunch within sight of the Grain and Feed. Clara couldn't have murdered her.

Colleen crosses Pine. A half-dozen mothers sit on the edge of the fountain with their dresses pulled up over their knees, legs in the water up to their calves. Children shriek and splash. Not unlike she and Charlotte dipping under the bridge, shrieking with the cold. Nearly blushes at herself. At Charlotte's nipple tape.

She sips from the drinking fountain to wash three aspirin down. The stitch in her side feels like broken glass. The pillow doesn't help. One chestnut gives some relief from the sun.

David Roy's Indian. Colleen was wondering how long it would take him to ride through. Going nowhere. Casting for Naughts.

Charlotte and Colleen had been swimming up at the Banks, where the bottom drops off and catfish troll. They had been fourteen and Charlotte'd dared her to swim naked and she'd double-dared and they'd just stripped to their nothings when they'd heard motorcycles on the bridge and dove under the water. They'd thought the boys'd seen them because they'd stopped on the bridge, but it was too far, they couldn't have seen anything. But they'd revved their engines and Charlotte'd actually squealed. The water had been freezing. Colleen remembers their nipples straining, standing straight out. Remembers worrying, covering her breasts, wondering how actresses in swim suits never showed. "Nipple tape," said Charlotte. Simple as can be. Nipple tape. Charlotte never had a baby, thinks Colleen. The boys on the bridge had revved again. Emblems, funny-looking, not like the Indians or the Harleys. Hadley had heard about a girl who was pregnant and who tried riding a Merkel. She'd also heard that it would work better if you rode in a sidecar. Perhaps, thinks Colleen. With deep-enough ruts. With enough speed. Colleen's hand rests on her stomach. Swallowing a scream at the thought. She feels her nipples rising, nearly caught with the fraying nylon. She hadn't known nylon could pill.

Roy's Indian still on the breeze, fading. Compared to lavender and grease, the smell of exhaust is almost refreshing.

Odd. Colleen hasn't seen Eleanor Hayes ride though. Ella told her Eleanor nearly hit 100 mph on her Chief. Faster than what Rovin' Frake used to brag. As if he'd ever been on one. Roy said he'd seen a Chief up at The Hollow. People think places like The Hollow will have white buildings, an arcing drive, and tended grounds and shrubberies like up to the sanatorium, but it didn't. Doesn't. It does have a Peace Garden. Rooms tidy and white. Bleached sheets. No one knows why Roy was so far north, though she can guess. Riding past the sanatorium until one or two of the girls showed themselves. An old line. "You look tired, gaunt, you wouldn't want the tuberculosis, now would you?" Unbuttoning. It worked on a couple of girls. Worked on Ruby Martin enough for her to spend a few weeks at The Hollow on her way to the sanatorium. Ruby never had the tuberculosis, but the sanatorium was happy to keep her for the cures and her grandfather's money. Of course one or two of the girls thought they looked fantastic, what with the tired and gaunt, enhanced with dark lipstick, near death, near ghostly. Femme fatales. Molly put sliced potatoes over her eyes. Cobblers. They were supposed to cure the dark circles underneath.

Colleen had heard they needed to be boiled first. Not raw. Irish Eyes. Robbie, when she was wee, told her she should mash them first.

When Grambly was first stumping for mayor in 1900, he'd stood in the square underneath the monument to Enos Nott and promised an open administration. He'd said "I know where the dead bodies are. It's time to air them out." There had been sniggers. The cemetery in the background. Two diggers leaning on their shovels. Not actually in the cemetery, but on the street, taking a break from digging out the sewer drain, but it'd amounted to the same thing. He'd looked like an idiot standing there and saying those things. Of course he'd been elected. Every town needs a village idiot, or so Rischel'd written in an editorial. The monument is still there, on the church side of the square, though the graves have been moved—and the "E" has been worn away by two generations of industrious boys—nos Nott.

Colleen realizes she's missed a few dozen cars, several cycles of red to green and back. She slashes away on the steno pad to catch up.

David Roy cycles through, dusty. Down to the river and across by the sound of him. The Braçir Belles keep the shine on their Indians, their Scouts, even through the mud. Scouts. Belles. Brown overalls with white pockets. People think their bubs are out when they see them coming. Sure, they smile for the boys. And laugh when they get up close. The boys turn faster than a bullet—doesn't matter if they stall or what. Those wheels turn when the Belles drive on past. Colleen's ridden an Indian. Felt it from her spine on up. Last time through, one of the Belles was riding double, hands wrapped and holding tight to the pockets. Tuber Nott wet his pants.

Robbie wants a motorcycle. Baby girl on a bike. Mothers don't worry.

Grambly doesn't like motorcycles. Neither does Hollis. Horse thieves, they say, hip flasks at the ready.

Colleen wonders when they're going to begin naming cars after horses just to irritate Grambly.

"*His* mother should have taken the 'drive to Rome,'" Marlene'd said.

"Couldn't. No cars then."

"Maybe she did, by horse, but it didn't take."

"Maybe that's why he hates horses."

Model T. Model A. 51. Reo. Willys Knight. De Soto.

Another Ford chuffs through. Driven by a Dank.

William was always pulling out his book. He'd said his father had ridden a motorcycle and wrote it all down. His grandfather Pierce had ridden a bay mare and wrote it all down. His great-grandfather had walking boots and wrote it all down. Every fall, like the clockwork. He used to brag that when he was riding out in the fall that he'd never had a flat tire. She can't recall any. The Limited had plenty the rest of the year. Those Goodriches couldn't take a nail. Couldn't take a rock. Colleen heard somewhere that nails were so expensive once upon a time that they'd burn a house to the ground just for the metal. Leave the furniture, the beds, the sink, everything, and just set it to flame. Surprising there are so many in the roads. So many they can't have all come from the horses. Or maybe. Pulling shoes while walking the ruts. And poor William just picking up every one of them with his Goodriches. Colleen thinks for a moment. She's never seen a Cooper or a Hardman or a Dunlop come up flat. The "spares" on the sides today are for show. Like the Roadster turning onto Main from Pleasant. Extra tires means extra fast. Sounds like something Charlotte would have said. William said that there were automobiles that had their wheels pulled off by the ruts. Not just their tires, but the whole wheel, right off the axle. Colleen thinks he was telling stories. Even then. Before. Maybe it was Jafferty or any of the other smithies tossing nails in the road. Or any of the horse dealers. That would have explained the pin-holes in the top. If the moon was bright, they looked like constellations. Counting stars as she lay back.

Robbie'd found her grandfather's journal. It had him motorcycling to Virginia and back, but William would have scoffed. His father never left the state, he'd said. William'd also told Colleen his father had a girlfriend in every town. He didn't believe it, but his mother did. So he said. Or so Colleen thinks he'd said. It was hard to hear him sometimes, arm dangling, foot on the floor, scream rising. So he might have said. His father'd never left the state except for at the end, with the crisis. William said he'd gone south, to New Orleans, smuggled "jeune filles" into Storyville, and died of yellow fever. Someone said he went off to the Cream City with all the Polacks and was killed in the Chinese riots. Another had him racing the prairie with Billy the Kid or Jesse James, them on their horses, and him shot off his motorcycle by Theodore Roosevelt himself, mistaking him for a buffalo. "Bah!" said Nils Öberg, bastard child of a bastard child, lifting a mug in Russell's. "He went to Sweden to father Greta Garbo," he sang, trying to come up with a rhyme for Garbo. Of course Garbo wouldn't talk about it, afraid of the publicity. Öberg. Working the road crews. Doing Grambly's dirty work. Shot one of Wilson's horses. "It was a deer," he'd claimed over a mug. Colleen hesitates. The crisis? That was in '93.

A line of very young girls walk along Main, arms entwined, chattering chickadees. They turn right onto Pleasant followed by several young mothers.

Colleen comes up surprised. She hasn't seen a bicycle all day.

William's father'd left his mother alone on their farm with a kiss and an "I'll be back in a week." He'd driven off in a flatbed, to Albany for a litter of French piglets. Bayeux, Colleen thinks his mother'd said. She says she doesn't mind surprises. She says she doesn't need a telephone. Colleen has another stabbing pain under her rib. Not this weekend, she says to herself, not with all of the ruts north of Moselle. Not this weekend, hand to her rib to catch the pain. Of course Robbie has a date. She's certain. Unless Danny has an accident. French pigs to Patrick to Cosette to Des. To Desiré. There's still time, she thinks. Shifts.

David Roy. Turning right onto Pine. Colleen watches the glass in the bank. She's seen the Indian.

It is hard to ride ruts on a motorcycle. Colleen had a thought once to buy one. At the time, she thought she might ride it all the way to Chicago. Or St. Louis. She might have been able to convince Molly if Molly hadn't married Hoge. Marlene would never have had the nerve. She recalls a bicyclist who took a steamer to France and rode his bicycle around the deck the entire time so he could say he bicycled to Paris. The Van Buren sisters. William had a fit over them. He'd followed them in *The Ode*. Rischel printed a story every week about them. New York to LA. Laughed every time he heard they'd fallen right off their Scouts. "Those ruts'll throw you," he'd said, like he knew. Colleen wonders for more than a moment. Could it be possible that the Van Buren sisters were Belles?

Robbie wants a motorcycle. Colleen thinks to Vivian Muldain. Zero. Her cousin Orenda Brandt arriving from Seneca Falls on a motorcycle of her own.

Colleen had wanted to stop there, to stay at the Hoag Hotel. She'd heard it had burned during the war. Everything had burned. Fires in the night as they drove. William told stories as though the entire countryside was aflame, apocalypse. That was the day a duck passed them as he'd sped along next to the canal. In town, a fountain to soak their feet in.

Vivian Muldain's mother worked at the Machine, making tools during the war. Perhaps that's why Vivian was so mechanical.

"Why do boys only talk about themselves?" Robbie'd asked while matching broken edges bearing Aribert Mog's fragmented face. "Even if they have to tell the same story over and over again."

"It was worse after the war," said Colleen. "After they had big things to talk about."

"Little things, too," said Mimi. "Boys on the phone." Then, with a quick correction, "Little Veld listens." Then, a pause and another quick correction. "I really shouldn't say."

"Everyone knows," said Robbie. "She listens to Danks and the Eldan girl."

"Isn't Little Veld married?" Colleen'd pulled a slip of tape from her thumb, folded against itself and useless.

"Pregnant, too." Robbie twisted a frame. Upper lip to lower lip. "Aha!"

"Ben Halloway," Colleen'd said as she cut another strip of tape, thinking to lips and boys and stories. "You're too young to remember. Austin, Hadley's husband was there at the end, in Argonne. Lightning Division. His brother, Ben, wound up in the same battle, at St. Mihiel. Maybe he was Lightning Division too." She'd cut another strip, and another. Lining them up on the edge of a plate. "You might remember. Ben couldn't move his lips on the one side of his face? He came across a rusted gas canister after the Armistice. Mustard or chlorine. He slurred his speech with the accident. He always sounded like he was driving around a curve just a little too fast."

Mimi'd blanched. "I hate war."

"'It was September 12th,' he'd start. 'It was raining. Dark. Water running everywhere. We'd been hiking for an hour through the mud. It was midnight when we topped a ridge, and there,' and there he'd pause, as if waiting for one side of his mouth to catch up with the other, 'there was the inferno itself, the entire world was on fire, flames into the sky....'"

Colleen'd paused to affix nose to mouth. She caught her fingernail in the splicer and let a curse slip out from under her breath.

Robbie and Mimi'd waited. Hands stilled.

Michael Payne limps past a chestnut. Joined after the Armistice but still managed to get himself a medal before Versailles. Colleen blinks. Same stories over and over. "...the entire world on fire, flames into the sky. The artillery was pounding the world flat. We couldn't hear a thing other than the roar. The rain picked up, but we couldn't feel it with all the heat and..." The sun suddenly feels good on her shoulders.

"That's nothin'," Robbie'd said. "That's nothin'."

Mimi had laughed.

Colleen had been at a loss. Nothing? Ben Halloway died after the war.

Face down in a bowl of soup, to hear Hadley tell it. Austin doesn't say much about the war. Only a few of them do. Collette doesn't. Won't. Except for the cooking. Bouillabaisse. Aligot. Béchamel. Niçoise.

And Racine.

"That's the way Danny always begins. 'Oh that's nothin'.' and then he'll start talking about himself."

Aligot sounds good. Colleen thinks it might settle her stomach.

*

Halloway's Oldsmobile takes a right onto Pine. Colleen spies Hollis spying through the plate glass. Ellsworth is driving? She double-takes. Des on the passenger side?

She fights a rising twinge of pride.

She fights a quick look toward the bank. Afraid for Des.

She makes a show of a slash. Her pencil grinds into the paper. The stab of pain under her ribs almost feels good. Warm.

Sara. Maureen. Gemma. Siobhán. Fiona.

The Oldsmobile turns into the alley behind the theater and out of sight.

Friz Rilla and Hans Gerron in a government truck. Conservation Corps. Volker had thought about it, but he was too old. Too married. Velda wouldn't have been happy having him away. Slash.

What do mothers think about when they name their children? Roone's Hatchery. Why would anyone name their son "Roone"? Rhymes with "ruin." He's the one who wanted the paving of the Leda Road out to the factory more than anything, lobbying the Conservation Corps, claiming the way it pots up is worse than any other road within twenty miles. Wanting it paved for the eggs. Riding the ruts? Colleen thinks riding the holes, more like it. The old lady Delano out that way still drives her horse into town every Thursday. She must be nearly one hundred. Still living alone. Once, William nearly ran her off the road. She had been ready for him the next time, shotgun blast of corn through his windshield. That's what he'd said. The old lady's a bit touched. Maybe not that crazy. Who'd shoot an automobile? Probably just talk. All he'd do was talk, arm hanging out the window. Just let it out, foot on the accelerator out past Roone's. Feeling the scream rising just to let it out, just for the joy of it. William had sworn it was true, that Lorraine was God's witness. He'd said she'd remember. Said she'd gotten a piece of corn in her eye. Swelled up a bit and turned blue. Her eyes tended to do that. After, Desiré took care of her. That's nothin'. Colleen laughs to herself. Says it aloud. "That's nothin'." They used to shoot horses. A draft left in the middle of Main and Front Street, just this side of the bridge, when the Runabouts first coughed and wheezed their way through town. Colleen must have been four or five. After the fires. Her grandfather had brought her into town on the wagon full with melons. Her grandfather's heavy had pulled up, stock still. Blew out. The draft had been laying dead for two weeks. The stray dogs and blue bottles had their way until the stink rose something awful. Grambly stood on a box and said the day of the horse was dead. His brother had just started selling Iroquois Runabouts and Model Ds on outer Main. He'd gone out of business the following year. They were *the* most uncomfortable rides ever. Worse than Pierce's Motorettes out of Buffalo or Ford's Model Ts. Colleen hasn't seen one roll through the intersection, but there are a few left in town. Hinkley, three desks down, has one. Nearly twenty years old.

Hinkley'd said to Colleen, "Why buy new when it isn't broken?" Rust, Colleen'd thought. Hinkley'd been opening a box of license plates fresh from Albany. Shined one with his sleeve and handed it to Julian over the desk as Colleen finished typing his permission. Julian is too cheap to buy new. Axel Rooke's Runabout is the prettiest, a year later than Julian's, made after Leggett & Co. moved from Syracuse to Seneca Falls. Axel painted his red with the hope of stealing Lorraine from his brother Eben. It's a beautiful sight, but it still can't be ridden. No suspension. Even painted red, those old Iroquois look like Puritans buttoned down for a prayer. Counting sins on the odometer. Did they ever allow their women to ride horses? Maybe they would ride in the carts. Probably not. Riding the ruts. Sex or madness. Sex *and* madness. Hysteria. What the doctors say. What Desiré rails against. Colleen wishes she and Hadley and Cosette had made it to Rome back when. A horse of all things. Emptying its back end right in front of the bank as its rider waits for the green. Slash.

Colleen's thoughts are just about to land on Lorraine when she suddenly straightens up, and says, out loud, to no one, "Look at *that*! Look at the way it curves around the wheels, my God, the curves. Makes you want to run your hands over the entire thing, headlights to running board and all the way to the back. Look at that chrome. I'll bet the dirt slides right off."

She catches herself. Madness. The driver looks like old Woolworth, eyes just above the steering wheel. She catches herself again. Woolworth must be dead. He wouldn't have driven a Duesenberg anyways. Ghost car? It doesn't shine. It *glows*.

"Why buy new when you can get it used?" Who knew? But Ronald

Hoge had a point as he took the dent out of a Franklin with his set hammer. Molly'd slapped him with her free hand, Dúil heavy in her other. Colleen'd laughed, Robbie's face had turned redder and redder, eyes tight, and fussing for a nipple. Old Woolworth would have said "germs." His answer to everything. "Germs." Didn't want to sell soap because you could just clean the germs from the old rather than buy new. That Duezy, though, couldn't get a germ to stick.

"Why buy used when you can get it new?" Sounds like something William would have said, arm hanging out the window, words sliding out of his mouth such that Colleen'd have to lean in to hear them, lean in close and suddenly he'd kiss her like she didn't know it was coming. Kiss him back and he'd have to drive with one eye on the road, foot to the floor just to give a scare, feel the scream rising right there through puckered lips. Screaming kisses he'd call them and give her a wink as he'd stop to pick her up for a ride. He'd never heard the true scream, the full-body scream. The scream beyond madness. Desiré holding on, bringing her back.

It had been easier not to tell William.

Her blouse has too many buttons. They're pretty enough, but they hold the heat. She fumbles with the next three, four, five. Doesn't dare a sixth. She tells herself to remember to walk down to Woolworths later. She blinks. Twice. Ghost car? She imagines the boys spotting it. Hears whistling through the glass. Then, on it in a minute, rubbing their hands over the chrome, seeing how good they look in the shine, in the eyes of all the young girls as they steer with the wrist of their right hand, left hand dangling out the window without a care. Too young to know they need to drive with their left. Colleen wonders if the ride is as smooth as they say. Jafferty's son says you need a whole other set of tools to work on them. Makes one wonder.

"Why buy anything when you can get it free?" Danny Barton's motto. Peerless. Slash. Said it like he'd made it up. Sly-eyed. Robbie's best to be careful, thinks Colleen. He's already been past four or five times since noon, "test" driving his father's cars, elbow propped over the door, eyes scanning the sidewalks, screaming "look at me!" Peerless. '29 DeSoto Coup. '32 Packard Convertible. The '27 Packard Roadster from last Friday night's the nicest. Two slashes for the Roadster.

William'd thought Colleen had the flu and was ruining his grand time, driving out to Halsham's Landing or Deer Lake, but there she'd been in the bushes on her knees. The tear on her back on the road to the Gap. The dust. It's a wonder Robbie made it. If Colleen never sees Blue Seal again. Coldest she's ever been. Freezing rain in West Rapture.

The fire truck sparkles, freshly washed, hose rolled tight, Kevin driving. Kevin usually works the hose. Dúil is proud as proud. Slash.

Houlton Falls. Better than the lakes, which are simply dull, like sipping on a glass of tepid water. Braçir had been worse than Deer Lake. The deerfly had been mostly down by then with the cool nights, but the mosquitoes were fierce. It'd been the mosquitoes at Deer Lake or Lorraine at Braçir. She'd been turning oo la la by then. Worse when they'd gone to Braçir, with all the French there. She'd said she could parle, but Colleen hadn't understood anything she'd said. William had just smiled and dove into the lake. One would think that with so many French they'd have been driving Chenards or Delagos or the Quebec-ers's cars, whatever they might be. William used to say that he had a family thing with the French, with the smuggling across the river, that his great-grandfather commanded the rowing boats through the night. Lorraine hadn't understood. Rowing across the Porcupine? She hadn't realized he was talking about the great river to the north. William later told Colleen that his great-grandfather smuggled with the Irish across the river. He's lucky the Mollies didn't hear him tell such lies, as if they couldn't by themselves. Colleen's never seen an Irish automobile. She doesn't know if they make them. *Sinn Féin.*

*

The soldiers came back one at a time. Left all at once, five boys walking out of town on their way to Rome, on their way to the war. Called themselves The Elephant Brigade. They hadn't wanted a ride. Ace Crawford, who had always been reminding everyone that he "Remembered the Maine," told them they'd be walking soon enough. And enough of it too. 'Course he'd never walked—in the Navy shoveling coal on the Indiana, nearly killed in Cuba so he knew something. But they'd wanted to walk their way out. Something about shoes. A few girls followed them for miles, a two-car parade of honking Fords. They were leaning out of the windows blowing kisses. One or two of the boys didn't even know what a kiss was. They came back one at a time. Mostly silent. Patrick full of bravado and bluster. Even Ben Halloway, who'd lost a leg, came back talking big. They knew what kisses were by then and knew what to do when the jollies blew them.

Hollis slips out of the door, whistling innocent whistles, shoves his hands deep into his pockets and surreptitiously strolls through the intersection, the length of the theater, to the side road Ellsworth and Des drove down. Colleen pretends she doesn't see. Has no way to warn them, but knows that they already know they're being watched. Twinges for hopes that Des will be careful. More likely, Hollis should be careful. Homer doesn't have an ambulance. Rome has one from the Rochester company. Grambly won't let the town buy one. A hearse is good enough. Quieter, too. No screaming siren raising the dead.

There was the other boy, Toby Curtis, who'd left earlier, in 1915, in September, a cold September, about the time Colleen and William were driving about with William Jr., just months since the screaming. Curtis'd left to join the ambulance corps. He didn't come back for nearly ten years—said he was having too much fun in Parée. Said it like that, Parée. Came back knowing more French than Lorraine—could oo la la better than anyone over to Braçir. Teddy Lang asked him about the ambulances, wanting Grambly to buy one for the town, but Toby didn't know but for the sirens. Ambulances and hearses, all the same damn thing he'd said. One screamed. The other didn't. He wanted to know where he could get a drink. Fell in with the Danks boy who took his father's hearse up to Lime and the Hideaway Hotel. Before the war, there were rumors. After the war they brought bourbon up from Kentucky. Had a regular route. Followed the old path. A black comes through every now and again, like the old days. Mostly walking, but sometimes with Danks. He ran cases of it down to Homer from up to the Falls. Patrick knew there were caves behind the falls and they could get to them from the north side along a narrow ridge. The caves were just behind the water. The falls were there because everything was lime and rotted away. That's why they called it Lime. That's what Patrick'd said. Colleen had believed him. The caves were big enough for a half-dozen cars. The walls were all crusted white. The floor was just plain hard. Smooth, but hard. Hurt Colleen's back something awful to lay back. Cool in the summer, cool enough for Danks to keep his bourbon happy. They were a ways from the road. The poison oak was thick enough to keep people out. People probably wonder about a hearse parked along the road. Perfect vehicle for carrying cases of bottles. A second set of shocks to help with all the weight of the caskets. A mechanic in Kentucky installed a V16. It still couldn't go more than 30. Too heavy. Father Danks used to smile to the women and say "Too early to take a ride?" and say it with a little wink, or a twitch, it was hard to tell. Hard to tell if he was just waiting for you to die or just die a little. Toby Curtis used to say that. "Die just a little" with his own wink after he came back. No doubt what *he* meant. "Hel*lo* Colleen." Doesn't wink much anymore, not since he winked at Robbie. People say he'd lost his eye in the war. People say all sorts of things.

There was writing in the walls, in the crust, in the caves. Love notes, some. Mostly accounting for the bottles. Slashes in the lime marking who owed what to whom. Bathroom humor half scraped away. La petite mort.

One screams and the other one doesn't. Colleen shudders. Forces her thoughts in another direction. Perhaps Saturday night would be a good night to see Cagney in *Hard to Handle*. Con artist. She could use a dose of Ruth Donnelly. Something to make her laugh.

Hollis has an ice from Spinelli's and is leaning against the granite wall of the library. The ice is melting faster than he can eat it. Makes it difficult for him to maintain his cool, his casual nonchalance. Nonchalance. Colleen gives herself an oo la la. Cosette would have laughed.

Dúil coos and warbles up from behind, jouncing Smudge as she joins Colleen on the bench. She hoists her baby girl Colleen's way. Colleen pulls her close for the smell of her hair, and readjusts her brim. Colleen's pencil falls to the grass. A page in her steno tears with the passing of Smudge, Aednat, little fire, granddaughter of a blacksmith, daughter of the fire department, of Kevin Branaugh. Smudge. Eyes tight with sleep. Dúil leans back, happy for the pressure off her back.

Grambly steps out of the bank, stares down Pine to Hollis. Hollis has dropped his ice and is busy sliding it over the curb without seeming to, hands back deep in his pockets. Whistling again. Rocking toe to heel, like Chaplin's tramp. Colleen wishes his whistling was silent. Two young girls cross Pleasant, arms locked, laughing, and out of sight down Main. Grambly steps inside with the first bead of sweat.

"Seen Halloway?" A smile begins on the right side of Dúil's mouth. By the time it reaches the left, visible to Colleen, it's all teeth, full-blown and glowing. Dúil knows. Knows that Grambly has her watching for Halloway, Wilson, Ellsworth.

"Not today," says Colleen. She draws Smudge even closer. Feels her all through her body. Feels a warmth deeper than the sun's, running up the length of her spine. A tear follows the warmth.

"Not today," she says again. Her own smile matches Dúil's, fades just as quickly as Matson comes over the rise, the tracks, and is stopped by the light. He spies the two of them. Almost leers. Grammar teacher. Robbie's never had trouble, but he flirted something horrible with Dúil. Followed her for several blocks after school unless she turned toward her father's shop. Colleen doesn't want to think about Rome, about the science teacher, she doesn't know his name, doesn't want to thinks about the math teacher, Richard Earl, but he bubbles up. Lettie Hayes, poor girl, thinking she's in love with her mathematics teacher. Holding her stomach. "I'm keeping him," she'd said, voice on the rise. Clutching her stomach. "Mr. Earl doesn't love Zero. He loves me!" Colleen squeezes Smudge again for the comfort. Matson turns right onto Pleasant and shortly thereafter comes back over the rise to the intersection. The light remains green. Dúil ignores him. Colleen can't slash, her pencil is still in the grass.

Grambly wants a new fire truck. La France isn't good enough anymore. That's not what Kevin says, but he's worried about losing his place on the hose.

Colleen believes she was five when the hotel burned. They could see the smoke from her great-uncle's farm in The Settlement, but not from her father's further north. Kevin doesn't know what it was like without hoses. When the hotel burned, sixty, seventy, eighty, one hundred men passed buckets up from the river. Men and women passing buckets. The hotel turned to cinder, but they saved the law office next door, Halloway's office. Woolworths was fine, of course. Kesling's Dry Goods was burned before they could hitch the horses and bring the water barrels from around the corner. That's what Athair, what Dhaedai, reported. Colleen wonders where all the buckets went. Where they came from. Tin buckets. Wooden buckets. Jafferty might have had the local children scare up the tin. He had them scavenging the ash for nails once it stopped smoking.

Dúil says it sounds like something Jafferty would do. Her father wouldn't have. She's sure. Asks where the fire started though she knows, has heard the story a dozen times from as many people.

Colleen is rocking Smudge and doesn't hear. Molly and Charlotte were from The Settlement. A quarter of a mile through a stand of pines from Colleen's great-uncle. Through tangles of barbed wire.

Smudge fusses. Colleen passes her back to her mother, feels the warmth dissipate, feels the twinge beneath her rib cage. Again. She twists to adjust the pillow. Leans forward to recover the pencil. Adjusts the pillow. Again. Dúil rocks her baby girl in her arms, content to sit a while longer as Colleen plays catch-up with her slashes. Ten or twenty or more. She misses Wilson as he drives past, on his way to Russell's? Conspiracies. Hollis misses him as he goes by.

Dúil laughs, quietly, to settle her little fire.

Grambly wants a new fire truck. Colleen's only a little surprised. The town has no money. Grambly was elected after the fire of '03. A new fire truck every two years. Something shiny to make him look good. Smooths his hair in the shine. Last year, Rischel ran several articles about mysterious fires over the past decade. Soon after, his outhouse burned, ashes to dust. Rischel ran an editorial on Hitler's jack boots burning libraries in Europe. On Hoover's secret peepholes.

"He*llo* Judy." Dúil snickers. Hushes Smudge. A boy driving an Oldsmobile. Sixteen. Old enough to know how to drive by the girls and holler like he's calling pigs at the fair. He*llo* Irene. He*llo* Esther. With a touch of singing. Can't do it with Elizabeth or Cassandra or Liliana. Too much for the mouth. Ellen's fine. Lily's fine. Ruth, too short. Same for Nell or Jane. "He*llo* Colleen," like that. Hanging out the windows hollering. Fords. Hudsons. Plymouths. Desiré said it came with the automobile. That boys can't be riding a wagon hollering at the girls that way. That the whole point was *not* to get the girl. That the point was to go by too quick to see if the girls noticed, if their eyes flashed with the call. The wagon is just too slow. Might be good for riding the ruts, but not for the "He*llo* Colleen." Maybe pony express, but who gallops a horse through town? Outside, perhaps. Country girls. Boys on the fly past their houses on their way to somewhere else,hollering their names like they were urging their horses to go and go and go. To go and get away from the girls as fast as they could. "Just a courtesy hello," said Desiré. Nothing to work oneself up over. Try singing Bon*jour* Desiré. Too much in the mouth with the accent and all. Oo la la.

Colleen asks Dúil if she's been to the cemetery. She's suddenly chilled, not sure why she's asked, not after Smudge's warmth. Not because Grambly has stepped out of the bank again. His eyes sliver in her direction. Toward Hollis. He licks his palm and smooths the hair above his ear. Smoothing. A threat. Four five six slashes. Her hand swings skyward and…*slash*. For the show. Hollis spies Grambly. Sends his own palm to his hair, mostly.

Dúil doesn't mind. It's been years. Molly had even picked out a name—Cailín Leanbh. She'd said she could hear her baby girl singing in the womb. Too ra loo ra loo ral. Swan song for mother and daughter. The stone says simply Baby Girl. The priest wouldn't allow Cailín Leanbh. Hoge hadn't known about the other cemetery, or he might have pressed Molly's parents. Colleen's heard rumors about a third baby cemetery on Settlement, lost to Saint Joseph. So run the ghost stories. Why else wouldn't Charlotte be able to carry to term? Rumors. The Irish up on Settlement say it was an O'Shea cemetery. More rumors. Every O'Shea Colleen knows says *Cac!* Colleen blocks her own stillborn, wishing Molly was holding her tight with the pain, two nights, dark, two days darker. Wishing Molly was holding her tight and tighter. Ghost child would have been twenty last month. No Irish Settlement. No one knew. Ghost child rests upriver, under the willows, with the others. Hush now, don't you cry.

Dúil is matter-of-fact. Her father will outlive her grandparents. He will be buried in the Hope Cemetery on outer Main. Slash. Dúil will have her mother and sister moved. Slash. Molly would be happier for it. Slash. Will be, thinks Colleen, not sure why as a single cloud passes the sun. Slash. Colleen's stomach feels suddenly cold. Slash. Empty. Slash. Dúil hands her a cookie. Unbidden.

A Packard convertible filled with screaming teenagers. Bodies everywhere, arms, legs flung in every direction. Grambly's threat—"I know where the bodies are buried." Doesn't everyone? thinks Colleen. There're so many cemeteries it's hard to miss the bodies. Fuller Towson. Packard Super Eight. Slash. His cemetery affairs. Every time he drives out with a new girl he changes cemeteries. There are more than a hundred. Have to be. Maybe two hundred. Lost cemeteries. Lost girls. This girl is from Cowen. Young. She looks familiar. Probably the way her ears stick out. Towson has a little William in him, a little Danny, with his arm hanging from the window. If Antonio Filli did that in his Bugatti, his knuckles would be scraping the road. Fool and his money. As was William.

"Westgate Cemetery has a new sign," says Dúil. "Building Permits Required."

"To keep out the Irish," says Colleen. "It's a wonder Hope Cemetery doesn't have one, too."

Towson returns. Brakes for the light. When William drove with his right and pulled his left in from the dangling, he'd drop his right on Lorraine's or Molly's or Colleen's knee, like it'd accidentally fallen from the steering wheel. Desiré would see. Admonish. William would sneak a smirk, just a little, so she wouldn't see, but she would have, in the mirror. Colleen doesn't think he'd figured that out. Or maybe he had. Maybe that's why.... Colleen catches herself from looking at the Cowen girl's smile. Like she's waiting for Towson to switch from right to left. But all the big-eared girls are like that, she thinks. Thinking about the ballplayer from Rome who left Robbie for a big-eared girl.

The Packard filled with screaming teenagers drives on by again.

"*You* were a screamer," says Colleen, leaning over, leaning into Dúil. Sotto voce.

Before the war, Patrick had invited Colleen to a drive out "to see the dead." She'd had the two little ones. Even so, he'd asked. He'd been planning to enlist. The Elephant Brigade. Patrick, Ronald Hoge, Austin Halloway, Ben Halloway, and Ace Crawford, but he hadn't mentioned it to her. Molly and Ronald had already married. Dúil was already a screamer. Just put her into the Overland and she'd start wailing. Molly couldn't do a thing to make her stop. Ronald would put the top down just to let the screams escape. Even in a drizzle.

Patrick had driven Colleen out to the Rooke Mausoleums in his Peerless Cloverleaf. Two-seater and fast. She'd had an idea of what he was about, but the cemetery had confused her.

Dúil, softly, "There, behind the glass," as Grambly peers again under the "F" of the First National.

Colleen tilts her head toward Dúil. "He likes the Irish," she says, with a brogue.

Dúil nearly laughs Smudge awake. A round laugh. An Irish laugh.

Patrick's grandmother had been in the cemetery. "Visiting," he'd said. They'd stopped to watch as she walked through, touching this headstone, that mausoleum. Then they'd driven around back through a thick stand of cedars, thicker than the rest of the cemetery, through an iron gate, to an open area full with mausoleums, crawling with naked women, draped at all angles, hanging over the top, arms adangle, embracing the names—Rookes all. Nearly two-hundred years filled with Rookes. Sinking under the weight of imported Italian marble. Sinking under the weight of money, senators, mills, sludge, siphoning, land, land, and more land, things that Grambly never dreamed about. Patrick's grandmother running her hands along the ornaments. Marbled ivy. Marbled women. If anyone knows where all the bodies are buried, it's her.

"What's with men and naked women?" Colleen doesn't realize she's said this aloud. Dúil laughs again with the surprise of it. Smudge burbles. Dúil, inspired, offers her a breast. Baby girl looks like her father. It's too early for her breasts to ache, thinks Colleen. Willing the ache away.

"Just last week…," begins Colleen. She'd been in the booth while Komár readied the matinée. *Tagebuch einer Verlorenen*. Komár had pronounced it a dozen times, correcting her *buch*, pinching her cheeks into a sipping through a straw, he'd demonstrated, she'd tried puckering, *buch, buch, buch*, a dozen times or more before he'd kissed her quiet. *Cabiria*, endless, came to a close, and he'd changed projectors. Louise Brooks. She had a beautiful bob.

"Your mother bobbed her hair," Colleen tells Dúil. Riding out in the

Limited, they'd all had bobs. Except Lorraine. She had two long braids. Desiré coiled under her bonnets. But Molly and Charlotte and Colleen had all bobbed their hair. "She had the most beautiful cloche. Black with a bit of green lace."

Dúil is thinking about letting her hair grow. Colleen thinks it looks beautiful, framing her face the way it does.

"Grambly," says Dúil, pulling Smudge close.

Slash slash slash slash slash slash. And another just because.

"Louise Brooks entered a pharmacy. The pharmacist had postcards with naked women."

"Tuber Nott had them," says Dúil. "He thought he could wow me with them. Said they were all from Russia. Shuffling. Except for the Latvians and Romanians."

It is Colleen's turn to laugh.

The Packard passes, accelerating again over the tracks. Over the rise.

"Folding cameras. All of the boys had them."

"William?"

"William had his Limited."

"Patrick?"

"His family works in marble." Surprising herself with what she doesn't want to admit.

Patrick had reached behind Colleen's seat and pulled out a blanket. They'd walked past his uncle, who had women embraced, arms and legs entangled, kissing each other, and suddenly, as though inspired, he'd kissed her. His lips were as smooth and as cold as marble. Just as suddenly, he'd pulled out a condom. Patrick Rooke and he'd come courting with syphilis. But he hadn't then, not until later, the war, and Germany. It'd been nearly dusk, and Colleen'd nearly screamed venereal, then thought she'd seen his grandmother walking in their direction, ghost-walking over the dew, and she'd found herself running, barefoot, because she'd lost her shoes to the wet, the war, the sylphs.

Patrick, madder than spit, must have driven the Cloverleaf over sixty miles-per-hour out to the farm. Colleen was still swallowing her scream in the dark, with the world racing by, and she'd just wanted to see Desiré so badly. So badly. She'd nearly vomited.

Lorraine drives past again in her Packard. She always did go for the red automobile, enough to have Eben pay for paint even if they'd bought it black. Eben had been driving a red Buick Speedster when he'd first asked Lorraine. The entire time she'd ridden with William her neck would be swiveling her head to anything red. It'd gotten so she could actually hear red coming. Anything red. A pair of socks. A bottle cap. Anything. William hadn't paid any attention. Not enough to paint The Limited. The boys at Russell's told him to paint it red. Anything. He finally had a small picture—a "tattoo," Molly'd laughed—of the Wright brothers' Model B painted over the front tire on the driver's side. He'd said more than once he wasn't driving a Limited, he was driving an Un-Limited. It could, on a level, just go. Hard to take flight, thinks Colleen, with a cumbrance.

"Why do men like cemeteries?"

Dúil finishes breastfeeding, burps Smudge, adjusts her blouse, quiets her hands on her hair.

Colleen feels an ache. Again. It's too early. She tries willing it away, but her breasts hold the memory of Des. Patrick. After the war. The anniversary celebration of the Armistice. Fireworks like constellations. Followed by the swelling. Followed by Desiré and her hand wrapped around Colleen's. The surprise when Cosette arrived. Madam Cosette. She would have said "the little death." Patrick died. The big death. Colleen hopes he rots in hell. His mausoleum has a Virgin Mary on it. Draped like one of Rooke's nymphs, but veiled. Cosette says his mother had it put there.

Colleen shakes off the thought of a Mrs. Komár. Shakes off Saturday. Leans into Dúil, Smudge, for a deep inhale.

"The ladies," says Colleen as Dúil gathers herself. Colleen slips her feet into her shoes. She hadn't realized she'd taken them off. They both rise, and cross Pine to the theater. Dúil continues on, to the fire house.

Hollis has disappeared.

Patrick never knew.

*

She rinses her face without looking in the mirror. William. Patrick. Komár. Thinks to Desiré. Dries her hands. To The Hollow. She will borrow Hadley's Flying Cloud. If she goes. When she goes.

Marlene hands her a glass of water. With ice. They stand at the register, eyes to the street. Little Veld is in the window pushing jacks. Pulling jacks. It's too hot for that, thinks Colleen. Marlene says it for her. Too hot to be behind glass with the sun burning in.

The Packard drives through the intersection to the river. No one bothers with the screams.

The Rome reporter, on foot now, walks past Little Veld, leers. Colleen is reminded of the pharmacist. *Tagebuch einer Verlorenen*. Duds isn't following.

"Lettie didn't do it," says Colleen.

"A couple of boys were in, saying Clara Shure will be arrested tomorrow." Marlene has changed cases.

Colleen scoffs. "Edwin wasn't that way."

"Why wouldn't Lady have known? Sitting on that bench every day." Colleen and Marlene have worried over Lady for the past month.

Silence settles.

"Woolworths has a nice pair of wedges," says Marlene.

Colleen finishes her water. Stops by the theater again, stepping into the dark. The theater is cooler than the street. The rows upon rows of empty seats are a comfort. She wants to sit, sit alone in the dark, to think about nothing, to feel nothing. To simply sit.

The whoosh of heat and light as she opens the door nearly knocks her back inside. She hovers on the door jamb, half inside, half out. Hovers a full minute before stepping on through, the glass swinging shut behind her. Little Veld is still pushing jacks, pulling jacks across the way.

She returns to the square. Ignores the clock. Removes her shoes. The heels are too high. Her knees hurt. She hurts. She wishes it *were* the flu. She takes her time settling, opening her steno, her pencil at the ready. Several cars drive through from Pleasant to Pine. She takes a breath, a deep breath that slides under her ribs. Exhales.

Ace Crawford's Franklin. His son is driving. Slash. Ace'd been scalded when it'd overheated, radiator spurting water like a fancy fountain. All of the welds had fallen apart with the heat. All anyone was driving then. Franklins. Those and a dozen or more Cortlands. Ronald banging out dents.

Rischel'd reported the hotel fire started in the kitchen, boiling pot of water.

It'd been a couple of years after the fire before the town could afford the La France. Every two years, Grambly sells the old one to Joe Wilson. Every one. Due again, says Grambly. Colleen glances across Main, but the bank's windows are empty. Perhaps the sun has driven them into the shadows. A block down, Little Veld in full sun.

The La France did fine with the Tennant fire last year. Four houses came down, but the La France saved the rest on the block, even without a water tank. The whole while they were pumping Colleen had been thinking about Lorraine and her oo la la. After the war, everything was France. Cars, wine, kisses, syphilis…the oo la la's. Motoblocs. Bugattis. Before the war, every town between Havelon and Niagara had burned at some point. Homer? Just the hotel. Just the dry goods. Rischel opined, "Why buy new?"

The convertible filled with screaming teenagers drives through again. Colleen thinks to extra slashes. How many times will they ride through before they grow bored and head to the Falls? Slash slash slash slash. It's still early.

The Elephant Brigade. Austin Halloway liked Bugattis, but Ace Crawford said they were just too damn small and winked as if everyone all knew what he meant. Seems like everyone had something in their eyes since the war. Hadley protested. Hadley's only ninety pounds, even now. She and Austin eloped a week after. After Kenna, they never had children. People blame her. She blames the war.

Sun on glass. Colleen can see Grambly's anxiety even in the shadows. Conspiracies.

Roone's egg wagon comes over the rise full throttle rattling the tracks, empty and returning from deliveries in Rome, crates bouncing in the bed. A Speedwagon purchased new by Morrow's son. Roone bought from him years ago. Rusting, though not so anyone would notice. There were rumors he'd give the woman Delano rides. Not likely, thinks Colleen. Jemmy had to accelerate when he drove past her place. Delano'd be waiting for him, shotgun full with bloody butcher. He'd broken a few eggs accelerating like that. Someone said she'd taken a shovel to the road after they graded just to dig a few ruts so the trucks wouldn't be driving so fast. "It'd help her aim," Hadley'd said, "if they were moving slower." More likely the Delano woman just wanted the whole load to break on those ruts. Jemmy joked about scrambled eggs, but it wasn't funny. It was frightening to see her setting out in her farmyard like that, gun waiting. And with no doors, there was nothing between them and flying corn. At least she'd had a reason with the egg truck. No reason for William and Lorraine. Unless she didn't like the Pierce brothers.

Of course, the Delano woman knew eggs ruined just for the shaking. Jemmy and Colleen had delivered a load to Sunderson's confectionery and Sunderson'd known right off they were bad. Held one up to the light, put it up to his ear, and gave it a little twist. He'd said the whole load was bad. Might was well take it to the bread factory, let them use bad eggs. No one cares about bread, he'd said. White bread. Shaken his head. White bread and bad eggs. He'd said he was waiting for the ergot to settle in. Then they'd come running for his cakes, he'd said.

The light cycles green to red to green and red again without a passing car.

The ruts were probably just the Delano woman's drafts coming out on the road. Grambly wanted to, wants to, make a law against the horses. Conspiracies. Desiré would have fought for the wagons. That truck was new then. Painted cream like whole cream. It'd been a shame to put the hatchery's name on it, it was that beautiful. The front wasn't so comfortable, but back, where the eggs rode, was a smooth ride. Robbie likes her Uncle Jemmy. They laugh at the same things. She wouldn't have liked the way he always smelled of eggs and chickens. Mechanics smell of grease. Butchers of meat. Printers of ink.

Dirt. Colleen thinks to Grambly and Hollis and the rest.

That egg truck used to be clean, spotless. Roone would have Jemmy wash it before it went out for delivery. Said he didn't want anyone thinking the eggs were dirty, like they had chicken on them. Jemmy hated that truck. William did, too. Didn't matter how many times William washed his Limited, it caught the dirt before he'd driven a mile. If he hadn't ridden out in all directions he might have kept it cleaner. It didn't take the wear all that well either even though it presented itself otherwise. The tires held. But there was always something. Suspension dropping. After the Falls, the odometer missed miles. Added miles. The gas tank leaked one time so badly that Colleen thought the road was going to explode. The faint memory of the smell scrapes against the back of her throat. She gags. Nearly vomits. Steadies herself against the back of the bench. She thinks Molly had been along, riding in the back with her. Lorraine in the front. Molly kept ducking behind the seat to let the match catch a flame. They'd been smoking Players, mostly for the cards, but the air had been swirling. Lorraine wanted to slap them. Colleen could tell because they were laughing so much, and William was laughing and not paying attention to her. Nobody could pay enough attention to Lorraine. She should have been an actress. Everyone would have looked then. Colleen can't imagine the Limited would be anything more than a wreck when it got to California. If it got to California. Metal strung on four good tires. How he loved that car. More likely he would have stopped in every town to wash it. It couldn't have made it back.

Jemmy hates driving. Jemmy and William. Vinegar and oil. The egg truck took it out of him. He moved into town and now walks everywhere he goes, even ten miles up to the farm to help his mother. Married Tennant's cousin. They have four children. The oldest is Robbie's age. That must have been a surprise. No pillow. No postcard. Just the scare. White bread. The truck is nothing but dirty now. It hasn't been painted in ten years, since the bakery bought it. The rust under the running board is visible from the bench. Someone is going to step right through it. Lorraine should have gone to California. She could have been in the movies. Like Mimi. Mimi has a bit of Joan Crawford in her.

Eggs.

Behind Colleen, six or eight children play ducks and eggs. She turns to watch. Their mothers clap. The children squeal. Quack. March past her with mothers in tow. A horse-drawn wagon carrying bottles from W.C. Morton's stops in front of the bank to let them cross. Colleen tries not to laugh. Tries not to think about Robbie as a two-year-old running naked through the cows. The children gain the sidewalk. The horse and wagon move through. Hollis runs out, yelling as loudly as he can. The driver drops his reigns and thumbs his nose. The horse bends its nose to one of the ducks. Lifts its tail.

Slash.

The Flying Cloud. Austin driving. Danny took Robbie to the drive-in in that one. It still has the dealer's plates. Austin hasn't been in to change them yet.

Double slash.

Colleen is surprised by another delivery truck. They usually run full in the middle of the night. Empty mid-morning and off the roads by noon. This one is Eddie Harlow's mostly-old ice truck. He used to take his old one out on the river, collecting ice in the winter, downriver from town below one of the old gristmills where the water spreads out after a narrows and a drop that used to power the mill. The water is deeper, too, and the surface freezes solid enough to drive over. Most times. Tup Winston lost his car to the ice six years ago. The crazy Rooke from north of Moselle had a factory motorcycle and would spin and whirl out there, cutting a groove until the ice finally broke under him. The motorcycle is still on the bottom. He survived. Eddie saved him with his winch. Eddie lives in a one-room house with no furniture other than a chair. No one knows how he eats. Shows up at Russell's once a day to deliver ice. Some swear by it. They break it up and put it in their water. Sprinkle it over potatoes. Best with potables, says Hollis. Marlene won't touch it. Colleen doesn't blame her. Town water comes from a mile upriver. Below that, there's too much sewage. Even below the drop. The thought makes Colleen queasy. A bead of sweat on her forehead with a chill. She yawns. Stretches her neck. Her feet feel good for being out of her shoes.

Two, three years ago a baby was found in the ice, newborn with the umbilical still attached. *The Ode* railed against unwed mothers, as though *they* are baby killers. Desiré had a few words. Rischel always could be nasty, even when he wasn't railing against Grambly. Half of the horse manure on the streets comes from Rischel. Him and Sunderson. And the Delano woman. None of them can face the music. Grambly had his boys fine Rischel for libel. Rischel's boys were ready. Charles. George. Lester. Especially Lester. Grambly's Ford was found parked in the middle of Westgate Cemetery. Every time someone misplaces a car, the Rischel boys have been out joyriding. They'd claimed they'd never truly stolen a car. "Test driving" is what Colleen overheard one say. "Beats the hell out of feces," said another. All four boys were standing by the fountain when he said it. "Beats the hell out of feces." And all four of them scraped the bottom of a shoe on the stone at the same time. Like it was a secret feces society. Charles, George, Lester, and the youngest. No one knows his name. They were the ones who ran wild last year. Colleen can't imagine why Robbie went to the movies with George. No one knows why Charles is courting the blind girl by taking her to the drive-in.

Beats the hell out of feces. Joyriding? Colleen knows some cars have been moved out of spite. Why else would Grambly's Ford be found in the Westgate Cemetery? Angie Piersante claimed a ghost moved hers. Suddenly, she'd said, everything started moving on her. The car would be just ten feet from where she parked it. She'd wake up and find the chair on her porch had been turned around. Little things. Beats the hell out of feces. Colleen's surprised Grambly's Ford hasn't been found buried in chicken droppings.

They say Eddie Harlow pulled the baby up in one of his blocks. Some said it was a girl from Rome who couldn't make it as far as The Hollow, screaming all the way. A dozen stories followed. Colleen doesn't believe any of them. She doesn't believe there was ever a baby in the river. Just sewage and ice. Ghost child.

Colleen yawns again. The sun isn't helping, warm as it is. She thinks about a cola, no ice. Hollis in the window. Ellsworth's driving Halloway's Oldsmobile around the corner again. Des not visible from where she sits. A left from Pleasant onto Main, over the tracks, and gone. To Rome? She wonders how quickly Komár will make it back. Wonders if he has other business there. Slashes a few cars. Mostly black. A maroon, filthy, white-on-black Maine plates front and back. She yawns again. Eats the other half of the cookie Dúil gave her. Breastfeeding. How could she have forgotten? The teething.

The theater. Hollis's eyes follow her every step, every pull of her skirt. She can see he's docking her pay, ticking away the minutes. Small-time slashes of his own. She blows him a kiss.

Marlene's. Marlene slides a glass of water across the counter.

"They've arrested Clara." Marlene. "Teddy Lang and Karl Harring drove through with her in the back."

"Just like that?" Colleen must have been in the theater. Without knowing why, she thinks to Charlotte.

A bead of sweat forms over her eye. Little Veld still behind the glass. A sudden lull in traffic, the light changing green to red to green without effect. A gust rushes her skirt, stymied. She shouldn't have worn the buttons. She feels the heat rising as she sits. She should have worn something with a larger brim. She still has a purple straw hat tucked away in a closet.

A half-dozen license plates all out of date, yellow on black, yellow on black. An antique—green. Colleen thinks to Patrick again. To Des. Des riding with Ellsworth? All the way down from Moselle. With Ellsworth? There is a meeting, later, with the man from Washington, but Des? Children in the fountain again, older children. Sitting on the edge, boys splashing girls. Girls screaming with the cold. Colleen doesn't want to turn, doesn't want to think about Charlotte. Squealing under the bridge while the boys stopped above.

Seven, eight, nine motorcycles. Over the rise, the tracks, through a green, and down to the river. Grambly doesn't want her to bother with them, but she slashes anyways. Grambly already has the count. She's surprised Hollis doesn't know.

Motorcycle boys. These aren't like their fathers, who raced out and who dug the mud with their bicycle wheels. Pilot goggled and capped. These boys are like William, riding out. Touring. Going nowhere in particular. Harley-Davidsons. Colleen is certain they are headed to Deer Lake. Colleen asked Edna once where they all went. Edna rode with Caspar Dank. She said she got her first cycle the first time she rode out. All over his seat. She's still riding. Had a motorcycle of her own for a short while. She wrecked it. Broke her arm. Nearly had the bar take her breast off. Dr. Ruben had a look. Once she uncovered and he had a look, he kissed her. Just like that. Blood all over her chest and he kissed her. Her brothers busted every window in his house. Scared the hell out of his wife with all of the glass. He left town in a hurry. Ellie down at the post office says he's in New York City now. Sends his wife a check every month. Must be for a tidy sum. She's driving a new Special Six. Every year, a new car. Trading up, she says. Last year it was a two-door Imperial. She's never traded up to a new husband. She seems off men, or so Hadley says. Colleen decides she will call Hadley.

Caspar's seat. Caspar'd said he couldn't ride it anymore what with all of the blood. He'd up and up given it to Edna. Colleen can't hold down the laugh. So many bloody seats out there. If they can't be driven for a little blood, they'd all be sitting out in the fields like the motorcycle on Cowen Road, with a tree growing up through the frame. Colleen thinks it funny where these boys go. To Deer Lake of all places, where they meet with twenty or thirty other motorcycles and don't do anything but stand around each other's bikes. Edna'd said the bikes were just penises. Just like that, she'd said "Motorcycles are just penises. Everyone heads into the mountains to let their penises out." Lorraine had overheard and nearly fainted. From that or the rye. Edna'd said that's why she wrecked it. Didn't know how to handle a penis like that. Charlotte had asked her if she liked the girls instead. Lorraine had nearly fainted again. Said "shhhh" as loud as she could. In the Limited all she would do was whine. The roads were too bumpy. The sun was too strong. The wind got in her eyes. They went too fast. Charlotte'd said that was the problem with all of the motorcycle boys. They just went too fast. Girls don't wink.

The Belles ride Scouts. Red. Four-stroke engine. Lorraine's head would be spinning. They don't ride to Deer Lake. The Belles are something, thrumming into town, and, as if cued by Hitchcock and on a Wednesday of all days, the sound of thirty four-stroke engines coming on through on their way to Tiche Gorge and the Hot Springs. They're a lovely bunch with their jumpsuits. The boys don't have jumpsuits. The boys don't have pockets. Two of the Scouts have sidecars. Colleen's ridden the back of a motorcycle, like Edna, and felt a scream coming, felt it loosed, whisked away by the wind.

A couple Belles wave. She can't recognize them with their goggles, but she guesses Dotty and Anne. Two others are holding hands, each on her own motorcycle, equally paced. She thinks to Tuber Nott. Smiles.

As they fade down Main and over the bridge, Colleen wishes she were on the back, holding tight, riding north to the gorge and hot springs. She doesn't know why she's wishing what she is.

Robbie floating, a ghost child. William never knew. The Limited. No cumbrances. William simply driving, trying to feel the wind. William Jr. with Jemmy and Aunt Bert. Every bump set her stomach, set his jaw. Colleen had never been so sick as they flew through the dark to Mare's Nest, clouds taking the moon so that she couldn't tell, north or south. Lucky he hadn't wanted the seats messed or he wouldn't have stopped. Mare's Nest. Colleen feels her gorge rise with the recall. They won't catch her headed that far again. West Rapture is her limit. Her gorge recedes with her resolve. She wonders what happened to Rapture. Ghost town to go with a ghost child. There's only West Rapture. It'd been bad enough when he squeezed the pedal and she closed her eyes and just felt it coming, up and up and out and nothing but nothing but a scream in the night. Convulsions.

And, with the convulsions, a cramping that doubles her over. She nearly falls off her bench. Comes to upright. Hadley. She needs to talk to Hadley.

An electric car from twenty-years ago. She'd ridden in it. Thomas Malcom's son driving now. Thomas was a looker. His son, more so, with his forelock and Scottish chin. A swashbuckler in an electric car. But the electric car never had the thrill, the speed, the roar of the gas machines. The danger. Pierces and O'Sheas probably killed each other a hundred and fifty years ago. Corbière's still in Ireland. America a distant dream. France a distant memory.

A week or more ago, Hadley told her that the new doctor, Dr. Karr, has a 1927 Erskine. Colleen's never seen one. Hadley said some of them have wheels with wooden spokes, as though they never could get over being a wagon company. Colleen bit her tongue. Hadley's Flying Cloud has wooden spokes. So does Austin's, even if they are painted black to look as though they are steel. Was the new doctor any good? Hadley didn't know. Colleen doesn't know anyone who's actually seen him. "Her," said Hadley. Her, thinks Colleen, who doesn't know what to think. She doesn't trust doctors. Dr. Lawall is a butcher. Four women have died in his hands, the last, from Russell's Corners. She worked the kitchen with Zoë. Zoë mailed him a box of meat scraps and table knives. He hadn't gone to the funeral. Hadn't for any of the four women. Might as well have been Muck Road for all the good he's done.

Maybe Dr. Karr isn't so bad. Dr. Tarfle is a son-of-a-bitch. Colleen wouldn't let him near Robbie, not even before her change. He keeps a woman "prisoner," taking takes her out for a drive every now and again and puts her in the rumble seat of his Studebaker. She is pale, looks like she is in perpetual shock. Johnny Taggot would have supposed she was from Hoofdorp, which shows how much he knows. Her name is odd, Wheat. Wheat for a first name. She might look like an idiot, but she is crafty smart—complicit, but not, as she subterfuges some of his evil, especially after the Alice Balme ordeal.

Dr. Tarfle tells all of his female patients they are worthless after the change. People call him Dr. Elixir. He has an elixir for everything. Hadley had seen him for seeing spots. He'd prescribed his elixir. Velda's daughter, Brigitte, suffered colic. He'd prescribed his elixir. Desiré told of a young girl who survived the elixir, whose unborn did as well. Born without fingers on her left hand. Musil curses when he sees Tarfle.

Colleen imagines Hadley beside her on the bench. They're smiling at a plain pink dress. At a pageboy. At a clutch. Hadley ducks her chin and leans close, talking out of the side of her mouth.

"Dr. Tarfle used to drive to Albany to get his medical supplies."

A maroon Studebaker, ghost car, drifts through the light. Colleen gives a ghost of a slash.

"That's where he was when the Shanahan family came down with the fever and died. Every one of them. Oldest child was fourteen. She was a looker already. Six sisters, all on their way to The Hollow." Hadley is working hard to tumble it all out in one breath. "Pity. They should have been on the way to the movies."

"The boys weren't nothing to see. Mud-infested."

The Studebaker has mud over its rear plate. Odd, thinks Colleen. Nothing but the plate.

"Wheat was able to keep him off the Shanahan girls. She couldn't manage to keep him off Alice Balme. Twelve. Dosed her with an elixir. The oldest two Shanahan girls wanted to give him a dose of his own medicine. Rumors. They syruped a valerian concoction. They tried to get him to open wide. They were ready to kill, but he got away." Hadley fights back an inhale. "They did get the Studebaker to open wide. Poured the bottle into the radiator. It turned to gum as he raced off to Albany." Hadley said that the radiator had to be replaced, but the doctor just bought a new car. "A Dank boy bought the Studebaker for a song." Hadley breathes.

Colleen wishes, without knowing why, that she could say it was haunted by the Shanahans. That would be a story. But no. Dank had it for a song. Still has it, or so she's heard. He hasn't licensed it for at least two years. She's heard he drove it to Philadelphia and back without overheating once.

Hadley doesn't know as much about cars as she thinks she does.

Grambly told Teddy Lang, Karl Harring, and the rest to leave Tarfle alone.

Wheat is still with him.

Funny things happen to Tarfle from time to time. Female complaints. The kinds identified on his elixir bottles. He's suffered cramping stomach, swelling breasts, urinating ten or twenty times a day. He's suffered nerves. He's suffered headaches. He's suffered tingling. He's suffered wretchedness. He's suffered elixirs. Wheat is still with him. She sneaks letters to Hadley from time to time.

Colleen hopes Hadley's Flying Cloud has enough gas to drive to The Hollow and back. The last "livery" is in Moselle. Next to The Fork. Estelle Rowen's restaurant. Estelle Rowen, who wouldn't give her a clean spoon when she'd asked. "It's called The Fork for a reason." Her mother should have taken the trip to Muck Road.

She stretches. Rolls her shoulders. Drifts once around the bench. Walks back to the fountain where she dips her hands into the water and rinses her face.

Komár doesn't know.

Desiré.

Smudge.

Robbie.

Colleen's exhausted. With the heat. With her back. With no sleep. With Grambly and his count. With accidents, as a La Salle slams on the breaks for a red light and a Peerless runs into it from behind. A love tap, Patrick might have said. Colleen might have thought the Peerless was driven by Danny, but no. She's recorded too many accidents giving out plates. Too many unrecorded, like the plate for the Pierce Arrow that Hollis's brother wrapped around a tree sliding into the curve at the Gap. That was a beautiful car until it kissed the tree. Bent the frame so badly even Jafferty's son couldn't sledge it right. She doesn't know either of the drivers, but they are out of their cars, yelling, ready to throw fists. Colleen yawns, tired with the heat, with being tired. The La Salle, blue with a touch of metallic in it is just a wonder. The richest blue she's ever seen. Probably like royalty. The smell of sausage sickens her, wafts from two blocks down, overpowering the smell of manure from the cow farm a half mile off. The drivers escalate. A small pool of gasoline spreads under the La Salle. Hollis comes out, yells, looks to her to do something. She tries to shake the sausage from her nose. Russell's, lately, has done that to her. The smell. She'd eaten there last time she'd gone to the farm. Fred Dean had been talking big, about Florida, about a hurricane, about a whole car lot full with Cadillacs turned into one enormous pile of metal. "Like a sculpture in the museum," he'd said. "Metal art." He'd said they had things like that in New York City. Colleen doesn't know that she needs to go to New York. Any more speed and the La Salle and Peerless might have been art. Fred Dean said they had things like that in Paris, too. Metal art. Colleen wonders if the French cars look any different from Detroit's cars once they're all piled up. Zoë uh-huh-ed him something awful as she wiped down the tables.

Slashes and more slashes.

Colleen wonders if the scrapes are art, too. The scrape on the Woolworth building down the street, where Lorraine claimed her foot slipped off the brake and onto the accelerator. It was a good story. Eben's Willys Knight. The brake and accelerator aren't so close. But it was a good story. She wasn't as bad as Kevin Heaney. He's fifty years old and never been in a car in his life. Didn't think he'd need to, he'd said, and talked himself into buying a Studebaker truck for deliveries. Like her father, he isn't newly fangled. Couldn't set his pocket watch. Had to take it to the jeweler every time he went out to The Settlement. Then take it to the jeweler when he returned. The Settlement never took to Standard Time. The clocks ran slow and slower. Every few years, it seems, they had to repeat a day just to catch up. Some did. Some preferred to simply let the clocks slide. No sense in fussing with the sun and moon.

Time. She has time, she thinks, knowing she doesn't. She can go. Visit. She hasn't seen Desiré in a while. Hadley won't mind giving up her car for a visit. Hadley might go—will go—with her. If she were in The Settlement, it would be different. William would have been late, running on local time as he did. Komár couldn't decide, can't decide for the drive-in, so he just advertises "dusk." Hadley can help. Hadley can drive. Colleen suddenly aches, back, ribs, stomach, a growing headache, full-body ache. She has to visit the theater again. Teddy Lange is directing traffic around the La Salle and Peerless. She steps into Pine without caring. A horn. A shout. She's on the walk and into the theater. Komár should be back with the projector. The theater is dark. A sanctuary. Komár laughs at the flickering people on the screen. "Shadows," he calls them.

After William left, after the war, after Patrick, someone from the dealer was showing a German from Mare's Nest an Oldsmobile, top of the line. He'd boasted everything, the headlights, the horn, the latest tires, shocks, seats, the smoothest seats of all, clean as clean, all new and all. He'd run his hand over the passenger side. Clean as clean. Tossed the German the keys. They'd driven Main, but the German couldn't work the clutch, hit the break, and lurched into the bridge. Both of them bouncing down into the river. Took four teams of horses to pull it out. The dealer nearly threw fists. Threw his hat. Threw a fit. The dealer said the German had to buy it. And the German said, "Why would I want to do that? It's broken." Of course it didn't happen. It's an old story going back to the first horse. An Englishman trying to sell an Irishman a cart horse. Wasn't funny then, either. That's when all the woes began. English didn't understand that the Irish already had their own horses. William wasn't English. He was, once, but he'd had it all bred out of him. "Alsatian," Komár would have said. "Germans know how to drive. Alsatians? Not so much. Too much schnapps."

Through the glare, sudden cloud making the glass clear, Velda has replaced her younger sister, Little Veld. Velda nearly becoming a ghost, said Robbie. So the story goes. Another old story and how it goes. The smell of sausage swirling the street behind the bread truck. Gorge rising. She ducks back into the theater.

The Harley boys return.

She's surprised her father didn't kill Gustav Martin. She wouldn't be surprised if Nott wasn't killed by Grambly, all things considered. Potatoes. Zeros. Robbie and Des.

Komár doesn't know.

Robbie and Mimi slide through the intersection, as she stands behind the glass door, the marquee over her head announcing Cagney. Betty Compson. She can miss both. Robbie and Mimi driving the Coupe around Teddy, through the intersection, past the theater, Marlene's, Lady's bench, to the bridge. Wrong direction. They should be returning. Not going. The wrong direction.

She wishes it was the Belles driving through. In the wrong direction. She would hitch a ride, up to Tiche Gorge, the dirt roads all the way, thirty-miles-an-hour, riding the ruts, feeling the scream.

Perhaps because half of his family comes from the Mohawk River Valley, from the footpaths, waterways, and old military trails, from the building of the Erie Canal and the laying of rail, from the paving of Route 5 and the thruway. Perhaps it is the steady stream of smoke tumbling out his grandmother's nose as she tilts her head back and laughs. **Rick Henry** has lived across the United States, but always returns to the sensibilities, landscapes, and histories of upstate New York.

Much of his fiction is set in the region around Rome in the fictional town of Homer. Colleen, in *Colleen's Count*, sits at the main intersection in the town in 1933 counting cars and worrying about an unplanned pregnancy. In *Letters (1855)*, a doctor is called from one emergency to the next until arriving in the mountains at a home for girls who are suffering a variety of complaints, all reported in daily letters home. His wife takes care of their practice and sends letters of her own, midst reports of the ordinary are extraordinary stories of babies stolen, a runaway slave, a hidden pregnancy, a fake birth, and a mistaken baby, who vanishes after a mishap at the fair when a lantern tips during a Fox sisters' séance. The central character in *Lucy's Eggs* is a woman beseiged by loss, but sustained by her flock of heirloom chickens through the latter half of the 19th-century. With the turn of the century, she realizes that she has become another person.

He was editor of *Blueline: A Literary Magazine Dedicated to the Spirit of the Adirondacks* from 1998-2009, is co-editor of *The Blueline Anthology*, and directs the BFA program in Creative Writing at SUNY Potsdam.

Other Works by Rick Henry

Letters (1855). Novel. Burlington, VT: Ra Press, 2019.

Then. Prose Poems. Chicago, IL: Another New Calligraphy, 2015. [116 pages, handmade and numbered.] ANC026.

Chant. Novella. Kenmore, NY: BlazeVOX[Books], 2008.

Lucy's Eggs: Short Stories & A Novella. Syracuse, NY: Syracuse UP, 2006. Winner of the Adirondack Center for Writing 2006 award for best fiction.

Sidewalk Portrait: Fifty-Fourth Floor and Falling. Novella. Kenmore, NY: BlazeVOX[Books], 2006.